The Healing Spell

The
Healing Spell

Kimberley Griffiths Little

SCHOLASTIC INC.
New York Toronto London Auckland
Sydney Mexico City New Delhi Hong Kong

No part of this publication may be reproduced, stored in a retrieval system, or transmitted in any form or by any means, electronic, mechanical, photocopying, recording, or otherwise, without written permission of the publisher. For information regarding permission, write to Scholastic Inc., Attention: Permissions Department, 557 Broadway, New York, NY 10012.

This book was originally published in hardcover by Scholastic Press in 2010.

ISBN 978-0-545-16560-0

12 11 10 9 8 7 6 5 4 3 2 1   11 12 13 14 15 16/0

Printed in the U.S.A.   40
First paperback printing, January 2011

For Kari and Kirsten,

my beaufiful sisters

and

best friends

for life

The
Healing
Spell

Chapter 1

HEADLIGHTS SWUNG INTO THE GRAVEL DRIVEWAY and Daddy tooted the horn of his Chevy. The dark blue truck looked like a bruise in the dusk. Finally, he was home again. And this time he was bringing Mamma with him.

My chest got so tight it felt like a gator squeezing my heart between his jaws. Drooling to eat my innards up and then spit me onto the muddy bayou banks, leaving my brand-new Montgomery Ward's red sandals floating in the purple hyacinth.

"What in the world is J.B. thinking bringing Rosemary home from the hospital? What a foolish old coot!" Mrs. Guidry talked in one of those loud whispers, like someone who pretends they don't want anyone to hear, but it carries across the room anyway. "If you ask me, there ain't no way a man with a sixth-grade education can take care of someone with a coma."

There was that word again. I plugged my ears, wishing Mrs. Guidry would stop saying it. Mamma *looked* like she was dead, but she wasn't really dead. More like stuck somewhere between waking and dying. As if her body didn't know which direction in the road to choose.

"Just old, traditional Cajun, Charlotte," Mrs. Martin answered, a pink flush creeping up her neck when she saw me listening. "It drove J.B. crazy having to leave the hospital when it was time for his shift at the oil rigs."

My gut wiggled like I had worms and I wondered if I should run to the bathroom now or if I could hold it. I wanted to hug my daddy so bad I was about to jump out of my skin any second.

I stared at all the vehicles sitting helter-skelter under the oak trees as Daddy parked his truck and cut the lights. For more than a week, an army of women had stormed the house, carrying a month's worth of casseroles and gumbo and crab cakes in their arms and stuffing it all into the refrigerator. Another flock of church ladies had arrived half an hour ago when they heard Mamma was coming home tonight.

I guess my big sister, Faye, could tell I was ready to fly down the porch steps and head straight for the truck—or else disappear out the back door—because she grabbed my arm with her long, skinny fingers. "You ain't goin' nowhere," she muttered under her breath.

"Oh, yee-yi! That hurts!" I swore she was going to pop a tendon. I hated it when Faye bossed me and gave me that look. Like she knew what I was thinking.

In a louder voice, Faye called, "Mamma's here!" Her voice was all fake cheerfulness, but the smile fastened to her mouth didn't match the worry lines etched into her forehead. Seemed like she might be faking that whole take-charge act, too.

"You gonna throw up, Livie?" my baby sister, Crickett, asked in a soft, breathy voice, her tongue teasing her jiggly front tooth.

"I ain't gonna throw up!"

"You look sort of green," Crickett added. "Like a frog."

I swallowed the nasty taste in my mouth and glared at her. "Any day now your tooth is going to fly loose like Paw Paw's fiddle string when it busts from the frets." I paused. "Or maybe that tooth'll just take a dive down your throat, and the tooth fairy will never know to come pay you a visit."

Crickett's tongue stopped wiggling.

"But I'd be more than happy to yank it out for you," I added.

"Stop teasing her, Livie," Faye said, sounding just like my mother when she was tired and told me she wanted me out of her sight. "I swear you wear me out. Can't we focus on Mamma right now?"

I didn't know why I was bugging Crickett. I just hated everybody staring at me, like they thought I was going to go crazy because I was there the day of the accident. Faye said I'd screamed bloody murder like some stupid girl in a horror movie. I overheard her talking to Daddy about sending me to a doctor. That made me mad. I didn't need no doctor.

Mamma had spent the last eleven days in a Lafayette hospital, where the halls smelled like puke and the linoleum curled up in the corners. One time when we were visiting, I saw a ladybug crawl underneath one of the tiles and disappear, so I used my toe to lift the peeling square. The old tile pulled up real easy—too easy. I couldn't find the ladybug, so I tamped it back down and stood on it so nobody'd know what I'd done.

Faye had fiddled with the window latch, but she shouldn't have bothered. I could have told her there wasn't any blue sky out that hospital window, only a brick wall. When Faye let a tear trickle down her cheek, the young nurse with hair like cotton candy, and lipstick to match, put an arm around my sister's shoulder. "Honey, your mamma can't see the view anyways."

I wanted the nurse to put her arm around me, too, and speak soft and sugary, but I tried to act casual on my linoleum square.

Those eleven days felt like eleven years—whole time I'd been alive.

And Mamma was still asleep. I called it the sleeping sickness because *coma* is the ugliest word in the entire universe. If I could, I'd erase it from the dictionary, but Old Webster would probably hunt me down.

"Gotta do the bed," Faye said suddenly, running off to get sheets and pillows.

I pressed into a corner, wishing I had the superpower of invisibility, when Daddy burst through the front door carrying Mamma in his arms like she weighed no more than a feather.

A nurse in a white uniform pushed a metal stand with plastic tubes and a bag of clear liquid. "This way, Mr. Mouton," she ordered crisply, parting the crowd. "And carefully, please."

Daddy laid Mamma on the clean sheets and brushed her hair across the pillow while the nurse checked the level of the bag's liquid. Every two seconds a drop dripped down the tube and through a needle into Mamma's arm. The tube helped keep Mamma alive. One of the doctors at the hospital explained that without the bag of liquid, Mamma would die.

Thinking about my mamma dying any second made my legs so shaky I wanted to slide right down the wall like hot kitchen grease.

Faye gave me a frown. "Don't you dare make a scene!" she growled under her breath.

I got the message, but I pretended I didn't hear her.

"I need those boxes right here, please," the nurse ordered in a booming voice, as if she owned the place.

I glanced at her name tag. NURSE WADE.

Her gaze landed on me and she wiggled a finger. One of her marble-green eyes was staring off at three o'clock. I'd-a sworn she had a glass eye, which made me wonder if she could pop it in and out or if she performed demonstrations.

"Young lady, you can unpack," Nurse Wade told me. "Put this card table right here against the wall next to the bed."

My legs felt stiff, like one of Crickett's Barbie dolls. Breakable if bent in the wrong direction.

"No pouting," Nurse Wade told me, then tried to sugarcoat her words by adding, "You're a big girl."

I'm not pouting! I wanted to shout, but I tried as hard as I could to be good and helpful. I opened the cardboard box and lifted out syringes, bottles of medicine, trays, bedpans, and bandages. I didn't want to touch any of it. Besides, how was all this stuff going to help wake Mamma up?

The first time I saw Mamma at the hospital, she'd looked small and helpless, her arms pinned down by the starched sheets. The nurses, whispering honeyed words, had given me tiny drops of hope. To see Mamma at home now—smack-dab in the front room—made the coma seem huge, like swamp monsters projected on Alucard's Drive-in Movie Park screen, which was so big it took up half a block.

Daddy straightened, clinging to Mamma's hand like he was drowning. "I thank y'all fer your help," he said.

The husbands sidled toward the porch, and I watched them avert their eyes. I wanted to turn away, too. My mamma was drooling, bare-legged in a hospital gown practically in front of the whole neighborhood.

Mrs. Martin touched me on the shoulder and I almost jumped out of my skin. "Run out to my blue Plymouth, *shar*, and get that last cake pan in the front seat."

I stole a glance at Nurse Wade.

"I won't let her bite you," Mrs. Martin whispered with a wink.

The cake was right where she said it was. I picked up the square metal pan, noticing that the cake had buttercream frosting on top, and ran back, figuring if I was fast that would be good. I had to do everything fast and good now.

The smell of the bayou wafted up the drive, followed by the scent of Mamma's herb garden by the gate. Sage, parsley, lavender, peppermint—and rosemary, just like my mamma's name—which made me remember that I'd forgotten to gather the herbs like Daddy had asked. I thunked the side of my head with my finger so I wouldn't forget tomorrow.

"Let me demonstrate the bed controls," Nurse Wade was saying as I slipped inside.

I reached the swinging kitchen door, then stopped so fast I almost dropped the cake. A female voice came from the other side of the door, sizzling my ears.

I pictured the women from church in the kitchen, clustered around the stove, gossiping like Mamma was laid out for a wake.

Mrs. Guidry's voice was tart as a lemon. "Don't he want her to have a doctor's care?"

"Nothin' else they can do for her," Mrs. Martin explained. "And hospitals cost an arm and a leg these days. Heard J.B. made quite a ruckus! Blankets flying, nurses screaming. He picked Rosemary right up off that bed and stuck her in his truck."

Mrs. Guidry tsked her tongue. "J.B. might be a small man, but nobody messes with him."

She was referring to the fact that Mamma was taller than Daddy although I hardly ever thought about it. Other folks sure did. As if a woman being taller than her husband was illegal — or something stupid like that.

"I hate to say this, Lynn," Mrs. Guidry added quietly,

"but it's weighing on my mind terrible. You think Rosemary will ever wake up?"

A hot tear pinched the corner of my eye as I heard the sound of dishes clattering, aluminum foil being torn and molded over bowls of salad.

"You think Rosemary's *dying*, Charlotte?" Mrs. Martin said in a horrified voice.

"What's worse? Dying—or never waking up?"

"I can't believe either option is better than the other. Think of the poor girls. . . ."

The cake wobbled and I was tempted to throw it in Mrs. Guidry's face, like someone on a television comedy. Except they usually used cream pies, and I didn't have one handy.

The kitchen door swung open and Mrs. Martin's face drained white. Quickly, she lifted the cake from my hands and I felt myself being hugged and kissed. I flattened against the china cabinet, and Mamma's wedding dishes with the silver roses trembled. Were those really the only two options Mamma had—dying or staying in a coma forever?

Mrs. Guidry bent down. "Do you know how it happened, honey?" The woman's nose was large and porous, her lips thin, double chin wagging. "The accident, dear. What exactly happened to Rosemary? J.B. won't say, though I've asked him twice now."

Mrs. Martin stepped closer. "Don't torture the girl. Can't you see how upset she is?"

"It's a simple question, ain't it?"

I clenched my fists together and dug my fingers deep into my palms, but I'd chewed up my fingernails so bad there wasn't any pain.

"Let's get our husbands, Charlotte," Mrs. Martin said, grabbing the older woman's elbow and leading her away. She reminded me of Faye, except much nicer. Shoes clattered down the porch steps, and I heard the rumble of car engines.

I stepped back into the front room, and the air seemed thick as old molasses in a dusty canning jar.

Nurse Wade tightened her lips into a thin line. "Mr. Mouton, you do realize you have gone against the doctor's orders? Your wife belongs at the hospital or in a nursing home. Caring for her will be a full-time job. You can't possibly give her the attention she will need. Feeding her any real food is dangerous. She might choke. She'll get pneumonia."

Daddy ran both hands through his gray hair. Even his face looked gray, like he'd suddenly gotten as old as Paw Paw. "Do realize that," he said.

"There are consequences to taking a patient without a formal discharge."

"Ain't plannin' on suin' nobody."

"But your daughters don't know anything about caring for someone in a coma—"

"Home is where she belongs," Daddy interrupted. "She'll get better here."

"I hope you're right, Mr. Mouton, but you are playing a risky game with your wife's life."

Daddy's head shot up. I could see him grab at his temper. "Believe it's time for you to leave."

Nurse Wade eyed him right back with her one good eye. "I'm not leaving until I explain about the feeding."

There was a moment of dead quiet, and then Faye rummaged in a drawer to grab a piece of paper and a pencil to write down the instructions. The nurse explained that Mamma would continue to have the feeding tube in her stomach and how to make sure it was working properly each day. Then there were instructions on bedsores and sponge baths. The list went on and on.

Faye's head was down and when the pencil suddenly snapped, I heard her sniffling.

Crickett tried to tuck her hand into mine, but I shook her off. "You're too hot and sweaty." I felt like I was being mean, even though I didn't want to be mean. I just couldn't think straight with her hanging on me.

Tears spilled out of Crickett's eyes, rolling down her face like rain on a car window. "I'm just scared, Livie," she whispered.

She looked lost and as small as a bug, but I couldn't even answer her, the lump in my throat was so huge. This was one of those times when I knew that Faye was a better sister than I was. I knew Crickett needed me, but I couldn't comfort her when all I wanted was someone to comfort me.

Faye suddenly cried out, "Look, Mamma's not breathing!"

One second Mamma had been breathing just fine, the next moment, nothing.

Before anybody could move, Nurse Wade stepped over and gave Mamma's shoulders three small shakes. Mamma gave a sudden gasp and then took a gulp of air.

"It's a simple thing to get her breathing again," the nurse said with one of her meaningful looks. "However, someone needs to be watching all the time."

Nurse Wade was crazy. There was no way I was going to shake Mamma back into breathing. What if Mamma took her last breath — forever — and became a corpse right in my arms?

"Do you see the risks, Mr. Mouton?" Nurse Wade's voice was sharp as a razor. "This is utter foolishness. I'll send for an ambulance to take her back to the hospital."

"No, you won't," Daddy told her. "We can sit with Rosemary 'round the clock, better than the hospital staff. Love and attention will bring her back, and that's all I'm gonna say about it."

A muscle in Nurse Wade's jaw twitched. She scared me with all that talk of Daddy going against the doctors.

I stared down at my bare toes in my sandals, and the silence swelled so big, I thought it would bust out the windows. A picture of Mamma floating in the bayou shot through my mind. I shook my head, wishing I could dislodge the memory like a painful rock in my shoe.

Looking up through my hair, I could see Faye weeping on the sofa with her broken pencil and notepaper. Nurse Wade was ready to have a hissy fit, and the church ladies were creeping closer and closer to the door like stealth bombers ready for a secret-mission takeoff. I didn't blame them. I wanted to leave, too, something fierce.

Except for Crickett trying to grab my fingers with her hot, sweaty ones, nobody was paying much attention to me. Gulping a lungful of air, I fled for the front door, down the steps, and straight toward the road. I didn't stop until I hit the live oak with its sprawling limbs floating like gnarled fingers over the ragged grass. I sat on one of the lower limbs, wrapped my arms around my knees, and held my breath so I wouldn't burst into tears.

I'd eat rancid bread, drink black bugs in my water, and get needles rammed up my fingernails if I could get rid of the torture movie of Mamma playing in my mind. I'd never had a bigger secret in my life. Not even the secret when Verrett Owens's sister Clarisse had to get married and his daddy hauled out his shotgun to find the "dirty bugger" and make him walk down the aisle with her.

Now I knew how Verrett felt, only my secret was worse. I didn't want nobody to know the truth about Mamma's accident, my daddy most of all.

I tried to pull her out of the water that day, but she was too heavy. I heard screaming, too, but I'd swear on a stack of Bibles that was Faye, not me.

I remember standing in the middle of the bayou, listening to ambulance sirens coming down the road, but I don't remember crawling up the bank or changing out of my wet clothes later.

I'd have given anything for that day not to be my fault, but I knew deep down in the blackest part of my heart that I'd caused Mamma's sleeping sickness.

Chapter 2

THE NEXT DAY MAMMA STILL WORE THE UGLY green hospital gown with the floppy strings that didn't tie right no-how. The color looked like snail slime. The front room smelled like snail slime, too.

Faye bent over Daddy who'd plunked himself in a chair and hadn't moved all night. "We gotta wash Mamma and put her in some regular clothes. Mamma would hate having a neighbor drop by and see her half naked."

"The whole neighborhood already did see her half naked," I said, picking at my toes from the spot I'd staked out in the kitchen doorway. Part of me wanted to watch Faye give Mamma a sponge bath and the other part wanted to run a hundred miles away.

"Fetch a towel, Livie," Faye ordered, covering Mamma with a sheet. "I forgot to get one," she added sheepishly, glancing at Daddy.

"We'll get this figured out," he told her with a sad smile.

Unfolding my legs, I got up and went to the bathroom, grabbing a bath towel from the stack under the sink. Faye met me halfway and exchanged the towel for the pot of water floating with soap scum. I dumped the dirty bathwater into the kitchen sink while Daddy and Faye maneuvered Mamma's head and arms into her favorite nightgown of soft buttercup yellow.

I watched Crickett stroke Mamma's arm and put her head next to Mamma's face on the pillow, whispering something in her ear about catching a baby frog on the bank that morning.

A clammy itch crawled down my arm. How could Crickett touch Mamma so easily? To me she looked like a dead person in a coffin or metal hospital bed.

"Better change these sheets, too," Faye said. "How we gonna do that without putting Mamma on the floor?"

"Roll her side to side," I suggested from the doorway.

"Guess that'd work. Will you help?"

"I'm cleaning," I said, grabbing a dust rag and the can of Pledge and attacking the china cabinet.

Faye's glare ricocheted back at me, but I ignored her.

"I'll help!" Crickett volunteered.

"Now let's hold Mamma to this side," Daddy instructed, moving her body to the edge of the hospital bed so Faye could grab the corner of the linen. "Watch them IV lines."

"I'll stay by her head," Crickett said. She pressed her nose into Mamma's face while she patted her hair with her chubby hands.

Faye pulled the sheets off the opposite side of the mattress and tucked them under. Daddy got Mamma onto her back again and then rolled her over the sheets to put her on her left side, but she started moving too fast.

I let out a yelp. "Mamma's falling!"

Faye scrambled to catch Mamma's legs as they tumbled off the edge of the mattress. Mamma's arms flailed as Faye and Daddy righted her again, but the IV stand fell to the floor with a crash.

Crickett began to cry, and then Faye started to cry, too. I dropped the can of Pledge and my heart thumped against my ribs. I pictured Mamma falling off the bed and smashing into the floor, the IV pulling clean out of her arm, breaking her bones, and throwing her into a sleeping sickness so deep she'd never, ever wake up.

Daddy shushed us. "Everything's fine, girls. Mamma ain't hurt. She jest got goin' too fast, like a truck with no brakes. Next time we'll go slower."

"Livie's standing there like she's painted to the wall," Faye said. "She could have helped."

I felt my daddy's eyes sweep over me, but he didn't say a word.

"I've been doing other stuff," I protested. "Like the dishes last night. And I wiped down the bathroom, too."

"Yeah, after Mrs. Martin and Mrs. Guidry mostly cleaned up after the neighbors left."

"Give Livie some credit," Daddy said.

I stuck my tongue out at Faye and she rolled her eyes.

"Suddenly, Livie's Miss Priss. Are you going to make us cookies, too?"

"Maybe," I said. I felt my heart leap inside my chest. Maybe my sister really could read my mind. I'd already inventoried the ingredients in the cupboard to do just that.

"I don't understand you, that's for sure," Faye said, balling up a dirty blanket. "You haven't stepped foot in that kitchen in a month of Sundays."

"I'll get the bedding," I offered, ignoring her comments and trying to do what Mamma always asked me to do. *Be a peacemaker, not a rabble-rouser.* I could almost hear her voice in my head.

"Already got it. Just take these dirty sheets and set them with the other laundry."

Faye stuffed the wad of sheets and pillowcases into my arms and I dumped them next to the basket filled with Daddy's muddy work clothes. I stared at all the piles of unwashed laundry—loads and loads waiting for Mamma, who might never do another basket of laundry in her life.

I pulled out the washing machine knob, threw in a scoop of soap, and crammed it full, leaning against the machine to feel the water whooshing to fill the tub. Two minutes later, the blades started to wiggle side to side. The noise was comforting, normal. Like a regular wash day.

Mamma did laundry almost every day. Mostly mine, now that I thought about it. No matter how hard I tried, I was always dirty from fishing, gutting, or cleaning out traps when Daddy was gone working the rigs.

Faye was always clean, always pretty. Always everything. Once I tried to confide in my mother. "Some days I hate Faye," I told her. "She's bossy and a snitch and likes to get me in trouble."

Mamma shook her head. "You do a pretty good job getting yourself into trouble, Livie."

"It's not always my fault," I'd protested.

"Sometimes it's hard to love someone when you don't understand them."

"It's hard to *live* with someone like her, let alone love her."

"But you still have to *try*, Livie," my mamma had said, not letting me off the hook.

Was I supposed to do all the trying? It sure sounded like it. I figured my own mother should love me as much as she obviously loved Faye and Crickett, but most days I wasn't sure she even liked me.

When I came back through the kitchen, Faye was opening the curtains to the windows that overlooked the porch and backyard.

Morning sunlight cut wedges through the tall cypress. Chocolate-colored water drifted slowly past the elephant ears at the bottom of the dock. Maybe the scent of the river would lure Mamma out of that darn coma. Get her to do something besides sleep and drool.

The phone rang and Daddy picked it up. "It's the boss," he said in a loud whisper, holding a hand over the receiver and motioning for us to be quiet.

"Yep, that's right," Daddy said into the mouthpiece. He listened for a long time, his head nodding about fifteen times. "Yes, I see. Yes, I understand, but that's my decision." Finally, he hung the phone back on the wall, but his hand stayed clamped to the receiver.

I hated how still he was standing, his head down. Then he straightened and smiled when he saw me watching him. "No more taking that crew boat out to the Gulf to work the oil fields, *shar*."

"You mean you quit?"

Daddy nodded, rubbing at the stubble on his chin. "Least I have to take a leave of absence for a few months. Don't know exactly how this is all goin' to work."

"Oh, Daddy." I threw my arms around his neck. That was the best news I'd heard since Mamma got the sleeping sickness. I hated him going away to work for a month at a time. Those months were times Mamma and I fought our worst. Going out with Daddy in the woods or running into town with him had always been my escape.

"Daddy," Faye said. "How you going to pay the bills?"

"Let me worry 'bout that, honey," he told her. He sat in the chair next to Mamma and ran his hand up and down her pale, limp arm.

My heart flopped as I watched him stooping over like an old man. Worry lines dragged at his face. His normally strong, calm hands twitched as he caressed Mamma's skin. My daddy looked like he was scared. Scared like I was. And that just made me feel even worse.

"I got an idea," Faye said. She disappeared down the hallway to her bedroom, then came back with a shoe box, setting it on the coffee table, which gave a lurch. One leg was too short and deep scratches marked the surface. Too many traps and knives and fishhooks thrown across it over the years.

I craned my neck. "What you gonna do?"

"I got the best idea," Faye said, smiling at Crickett and pretending she hadn't heard me. "I hate seeing Mamma lying here looking so terrible. If a neighbor dropped by, she'd want to run and hide. Only she can't, so *we're* going to fix her up real pretty."

Faye was well supplied. There was face wash, cotton balls, moisturizing lotion, eye shadows, lipsticks, cheek rouge, the works. "If you're gonna hang around, Livie," she said, not even looking in my direction, "then come over and help."

I thought about putting lip gloss on Mamma's cold, dead lips and shook my head. "I don't go near that face junk."

"Am I big enough to help put on Mamma's makeup?" Crickett asked, hopping back and forth from foot to foot.

"'Course, honey, but you do what I say," Faye told her. "And try not to spill anything."

Daddy rose with a grunt. "I'll let you girls do your makeup magic while I get me a cup and take a load off my feet." He shuffled into the kitchen and settled at the table with a demitasse.

I set down my dust rag and sidled along the edge of the couch, keeping quiet, but I was curious to see what Faye was going to do. Mamma usually wore a bit of cherry lipstick after breakfast, adding more makeup if she was going into town to shop. Since the accident, Mamma's face was pale and splotchy, her lips colorless like a corpse. She didn't even look real anymore.

I stopped three feet from the hospital bed and gave a shudder when Mamma's legs started to jerk. I backed up as fast as I could, my head spinning like I'd just gotten off a roller coaster.

"Olivia Marie Mouton!" Faye exploded. "Mamma ain't going to bite! She can't even open her eyes."

"Leave Livie be," Daddy told Faye mildly through the doorway. "She's gonna do things in her own time."

Faye bit at her lips, ignoring me again, even when I clutched at my queasy stomach. I swear she had no heart. "Crickett, can you get me two warm washcloths?"

"I'll do it," I said, running out of the room before Crickett could beat me to it. I needed to get out of there. I couldn't stand watching Faye rub rouge on Mamma's cheeks like she was in the funeral home getting her ready for the viewing. Sarah LeBlanc at school told me once that they put makeup on dead people so it looks like they're just sleeping in their caskets. Saves the mourners from fainting in the church aisles. She should know. Her uncle is a mortician.

In the bathroom, I ran water in the sink until it

got warm, then twisted the washcloths tight so they wouldn't drip on the carpet. When I got back to the front room, I halted behind the overstuffed chair, like a brick wall had suddenly sprung up in front of my face. I was pretty sure that if I got close to that hospital bed again, I might faint.

"Does Crickett need to come fetch them washcloths from you?" Faye's voice was a darning needle, all pointy edges.

"The coma isn't contagious," Crickett whispered, stupid tears welling in her eyes again.

My throat hurt like a marble had lodged inside. "Quit cryin' crocodile tears!"

"They're not crocodile tears!" Crickett said, weeping even louder. "They're real. You're so mean."

"Livie!" Faye cried out. "Crickett ain't done nothing to you!"

Daddy glanced up from his coffee, and my stomach sank when I met his eyes.

"Sorry, Crickett," I muttered.

She wiped at her face and gave a hiccup as Faye pulled out another tube. "I've got some super-duper Apricot Scrub."

"Let me do some gooey stuff," Crickett pleaded.

Faye squirted a half-dollar dab into her palm. "It's got apricot and nuts to make your skin soft and smooth."

Crickett ran her fingers through the creamy glob and gave Faye a wobbly smile. "Am I still going to kindergarten after the summer?"

"Kindergarten's not required," I told her, tempted to run out the door but knowing I'd get yelled at for leaving all the work to them. "You can stay home if you want."

"I don't want to be called Aimee if I do have to go to school. I want to be Crickett, with two t's, like a real name, not an insect."

"What if the kids tease you?" Faye asked, inspecting the box of lipsticks.

"I'll beat 'em up for you," I offered.

Crickett's eyes widened. "You will?"

"Yep, but if I'm your bodyguard, you have to be my slave."

"Stop teasing her, Livie."

I stuck out my tongue again.

"You are so immature," Faye reprimanded, like she was a teacher.

Daddy slurped his hot coffee, thick arms leaning over the cup. "How does crawfish gumbo for supper grab you girls?"

"Grabs me good, Daddy," I whispered, trying to hide the tears smarting behind my eyelids.

"We'll unload the traps on the way to school."

"I gotta go to school?"

"I hear it's the last day. Don't you want to say good-bye?"

I shrugged. I sure didn't want everybody looking at me with their sorry faces, but going to school was an excuse to get away from the house.

Daddy pushed back from the table and set his cup in the sink. "Faye, you all right for a little while?"

Faye didn't reply at first, and I suddenly wondered if being alone with Mamma scared my older sister, too. Finally, she nodded. "I suppose Livie should finish out the year."

Crickett clapped her hands together. "Come see, come see! We're all done fixing up Mamma!"

She grabbed my hand, trying to pull me closer, but I shook my head and stayed in the doorway. "I can see just fine from here."

Crickett made a face at me and took Daddy's hand instead, walking him to Mamma's side to admire the makeup job.

"How does she look?" Faye said, finishing the final touches of Mamma's blue eye shadow and the dark eyeliner. Her lashes had been brushed with mascara, and her skin looked pinker, not gray like skeleton bones.

Daddy took Mamma's pale hand in his large brown one, then turned it over and kissed her palm. "She's beautiful, girls. Jest beautiful."

"You like it, Daddy?" Crickett asked.

"Sure thing. Best of all, when Mamma wakes up again, she will love lookin' so pretty."

I had to admit, it was true. Mamma was beautiful. She always had been. The makeup was good at hiding the accident, too. Mamma looked almost normal again, except for the bandage around her head. And not opening her eyes. Or speaking. And flopping around on the bed like she was having seizures.

I couldn't look at her any longer without going crazy, so I made for the kitchen, then kept on going through to the galerie. Daddy had created a summer bedroom for me and Crickett out of one end of the long galerie porch. Sharing a room was okay, except when Crickett turned sideways in bed and kicked me in the shins.

A breeze swept through the mesh screens, and I took in a gulp of fresh air. Our house smelled like medicine and sick people, and I hated it. I sat on the bed and yanked on a pair of socks, even though I'd worn them yesterday, and tied my school shoes.

"Ugh," I said, glancing at the mirror over the dresser. I hadn't brushed out my braids, so my hair was scraggly from sleeping. My mouth looked like I'd been sucking on a lemon, but I didn't care.

The moment I ran down the steps into the backyard, a feeling of relief swept over me, as if I could breathe normal again.

Daddy sat himself down in my pirogue tied to the dock. "Let's skip across the bayou and git us those traps buried in the mud over there."

I hesitated, then said, "Sure you don't want to take your own skiff, Daddy?"

"Yours'll work jest fine. We ain't goin' far, and I hate to use the gasoline."

I bit my lip as he picked up the pole, then finally stepped in, sitting stiffly across from him. It felt strange to touch the polished wood, feel the hard seat underneath me. Daddy had hollowed the boat out of an old cypress log for my birthday last year, and I thought it was perfect. I used it every day, too, until three weeks ago. Sad thing was, the pirogue was still perfect, and I still loved it, in spite of what happened. And I was pretty sure I wasn't supposed to enjoy it anymore after what I'd done.

Daddy nodded at me and I untied the ropes, then pushed off from the dock where the waxy, green elephant ears hugged the edge of the bayou, holding the mud together so the backyard didn't fall into the river after the spring storms.

"Where's that paddle I made you?" Daddy asked.

I glanced away, shrugging my shoulders. "Lost it in the bayou."

I felt his eyes studying me, but he didn't ask any more questions. He'd been gone so much while Mamma was in the hospital, I hoped he'd think I really had lost my paddle instead of hiding it in the woodshed. Now I had to learn how to pole the pirogue, even though it was harder and took a lot more muscle. I planned to grow the biggest muscles I could.

An image of that paddle flashed through my brain. Maybe I should check and make sure nobody could find it under the stacks of firewood. My breath caught as I wondered if there were any clues on the paddle that would give my secret away.

"Jest sit back and relax, Sugar Bee," Daddy said as he stood up to navigate across the lazy water.

I felt the tension inside my chest ease up. Daddy always seemed to know just what to say to make me feel better.

The sun blazed overhead. Felt like cane syrup boiling on the stove. Cicadas razed the air. A bluegill flew out of the water, then plopped softly back under the surface.

At the far edge where the cypress knees rose from the shallow water, Daddy dug the pole into the mud and came to a halt.

I hung on to a low branch to keep the boat from shifting while Daddy pulled up two traps from the murky darkness. The wire baskets were loaded with churning, squirming crawfish. I clapped my hands to my knees while Daddy gave me a quick grin.

"Sugar Bee, we sure are gonna be eating good."

I held open the burlap sack while he dumped them inside. Claws snapped as the crawfish tried to escape. As I tied the opening, Daddy refilled the traps with bait and let them sink down into the water again.

"Water's low enough I can feel 'em down there," he said, poking the pole into the mud.

"Isn't that good?"

"Hope so. Gotta make our livin' off the bayou now. Till Mamma comes back to us."

I thought about his words. Was Mamma just away somewhere for a while? Was she dreaming inside her head? Could she hear what we said? Could she think any thoughts? I tried to picture my mother lying in that hospital bed for years—maybe forever—and felt a stone scrape my ribs and sink to the bottom of my heart.

That person lying in the front room was just a shell of the real mamma that cooked the best gumbo on the bayou, made flapjacks for breakfast, and painted watercolor pictures in her art cottage under the oak trees.

I rubbed my eyes with the back of my hand. Funny

how I missed those things when I'd spent most of my whole life fighting with her.

When I was little, I wondered if I'd been adopted. Until the day Mémère showed me pictures of Daddy when he was a boy. "You's the spittin' image of your daddy," she'd told me.

After that I stopped worrying, but it didn't mean I magically started getting along with my mamma.

"We can eat off the bayou," I told Daddy. "I'll get my twenty-two oiled up. That'll work, won't it?"

He nodded. "There's so much food out here, we'll be livin' too much better."

Daddy headed toward town and his salty gray hair ruffled in the wind. He looked solid as a rock. His thick hands poled the boat like we were floating in a teacup across a bathtub instead of the bayou.

I felt his eyes on my face, but I pretended I didn't see him watching me.

"Anything you want to talk about, Sugar Bee?" he asked.

The roaring in my ears was like a swarm of cicadas taking over my brain. I shook my head and stared down at the water, trying to stay still so Daddy couldn't see me wriggling inside. The secret grew in my mind, but there were some things I'd never tell another living soul.

Some people went to confession with Father John every week, but Daddy said children younger than twelve didn't have to go. It was too late for confession anyway.

I'd already decided that some sins were so dangerous they were better left hidden.

Chapter 3

ALL TWENTY HEADS SWIVELED AROUND AS I
stepped inside Room 17 at Bayou Bridge Elementary.

The smell of Comet was strong and hung in the air like a curtain. Last-day excitement buzzed. Kids drowned paper towels in the corner sink to scrub their desktops. Stacks of papers, old tests, and notebooks lay scattered everywhere. Piles of textbooks teetered under the windows.

I tried to walk to my desk in the second row, but Miss Beaumont caught me first and engulfed me in a hug. "Livie, you're back. We've missed you! I've got a casserole to bring over tonight, but I didn't know I'd be seeing you today. I'm so pleased."

I shrugged. Seemed like my tongue had stopped working. "We got a lot of casseroles," I finally managed to mutter.

My teacher gave a laugh. A smudge of red lipstick stained her front tooth. "I'm sure you do, honey. Maybe

I'll change that to a batch of cookies. We're just so worried about y'all," she added in a whisper. "Okay, scoot on over and get your desk cleaned out."

It felt strange to be back. Like I'd been gone longer than just a few days. The classroom was familiar in an old, tired way, as if I'd grown past it already. After summer was over I'd be starting seventh grade. Right now, I just wanted to get my old papers and then run away into the bayou for a week with my sleeping bag and a fishing pole.

Behind me, someone whispered, "I hear her mamma's laid out in the front room like a corpse."

I whirled around and my fingers curled into a fist. "Shut up," I said into the silence.

"We didn't do nothing," Sarah LeBlanc said primly. "We're just speaking the truth."

"You want to know the truth?" I heard myself say before I could stop. "Truth is, I'll punch your nose straight into your brain."

Sarah's mouth dropped and she wailed, "Miss Beaumont!"

"For goodness' sake, I think we can get along on the last day of school," Miss Beaumont said, shooing us apart.

"Come on, Livie," Jeannie told me, linking her arm in mine. "I'm almost done with your desk."

I breathed in the familiar sight of Jeannie's braided dark hair hanging against her white blouse. A gold cross dangled around her neck, making me think of my mother's crucifix chain that had broken the week before the accident. Daddy had mended the clasp with his pliers, but I didn't know where it had ended up. Maybe Mamma's jewelry box.

"Hey," Jeannie said.

"Hey," I whispered back. "You *are* here." I was so glad to see her I felt like crying. Then I blurted, "Eww, you're wearing lip gloss!"

Jeannie's hand flew to her mouth.

"It's *pink*."

"Yeah," Jeannie admitted, rubbing a hand across her mouth.

"What's next? Charm school?"

"Don't say those words!"

Our mothers had been threatening to enroll us in Miss Simpson's White Gloves and Party Manners Charm School on our twelfth birthdays in July. Jeannie and I had been born in the same hospital only one day apart. Almost like twins. Like having another sister, only better.

I noticed that Jeannie had already wiped down my desktop and stacked all my notebooks. I wished I'd put up more of a fight about coming. What did I need school for anyway? I could already read any book the librarian gave me, and besides, I didn't need books if I was going to be a hunter. Gators don't care if you can spell *paradoxical* or multiply three-fourths by one-eighth.

Plopping down in my seat, I tried to look over the stack of papers to decide what to keep and what to throw away. I wished I was out in the woods with my gun right now. My hand crept to my chest, and I rubbed the center where it hurt. I swear my heart had a hole in it, and if the cork popped out, I'd gush blood.

I swept the pile of old work sheets off my desk and into the trash bin. I wasn't sure I cared about the perfect one hundreds or smiling faces that Miss Beaumont drew at the top in purple ink. Mamma was pleased when I brought home good report cards, but I think that was the only thing she liked about me. Most days I was getting into trouble for dragging mud across the kitchen floor or enduring a scolding for forgetting my chores when I was out fishing for dinner. I'd figured out that bringing home a line of catfish wasn't as important as Crickett stirring the gumbo pot or Faye sewing a new skirt.

When the three o'clock bell rang, I dragged myself home along the road. Maybe Mamma would be sitting up and eating strawberry shortcake. Or painting in her art cottage. Or weeding the squash. I wouldn't even mind if she dragged me shopping with her. I'd go willingly. I'd surprise her. I'd be the daughter she'd always wanted me to be.

Instead, Mamma was throwing up. A spoonful of applesauce was in a bowl on the floor, and Daddy was wiping her mouth with a damp rag.

"She looks so thin," he said with a sigh. "I thought mebbe half a teaspoon of applesauce wouldn't hurt, but it won't go down her throat at all."

"You think Nurse Wade was right, Daddy?" Faye asked, a scared look on her face.

"Much as I hate to admit it, I guess so. And Lord knows, I don't want to hurt her or give her pneumonia."

Mamma made another gagging noise, and Crickett started to whimper.

"Leave the room, girls," Daddy ordered quietly.

Faye grabbed Crickett by the hand and I followed, not looking back. I was going to have nightmares from watching Mamma's body racked with those horrible spasms.

The windows were open, and I could still hear the awful sound of puking as I sat on the porch railing, poking my toe at a splintered plank. Heavy gray clouds hung like damp laundry.

Crickett leaned against Faye's shoulder as they sat side by side in the porch swing. Raindrop-sized tears sat on the bottom of Crickett's eyelids. She looked up at Faye. "Think Mamma's gonna die?"

My stomach clenched into a ball. Now Crickett was saying it, too, just like Mrs. Guidry. I squeezed my eyes shut, wishing I wasn't sitting here listening to my mother getting sick. Wishing I could sink into the floorboards of the porch and disappear.

"We must believe that Mamma will get better," Faye said like she was quoting Mrs. Martin or Nurse Wade. Then she whispered, "Try not to worry, Crickett baby."

I didn't dare say a word. If I opened my mouth, I might start screaming, and they'd lock me up inside a mental hospital. Or prison. Inside the house, I could hear Daddy cleaning Mamma up, changing her clothes.

Glancing at Faye and Crickett sitting snuggled up together, I bit my cheek to hold back the sting of rising tears. I remembered when Faye used to snuggle with me when I was younger, before Crickett came along. Then she started pushing me away when I came home smelling like crab bait. Or squirrel guts, when I helped Daddy skin 'em after a day of shooting in the woods.

Faye gave a sigh and stopped rocking. "Think Travis will call today?"

Crickett clapped her hands. "Oh, I hope, hope, hope Travis calls!"

Faye smiled and kissed the tip of her tiny diamond engagement ring.

I turned away, disgusted. Faye kissed that ring all the time. She said the ring was the next best thing to kissing Travis Boudreaux. Travis was gone to boot camp in Biloxi, Mississippi. I figured that engagement ring was covered in about a million germs by now and probably needed to be quarantined.

"You gonna have fireworks for your wedding?" Crickett asked.

"Can't have Fourth of July without fireworks, can we? Especially if it's my wedding day!"

I thought Independence Day was a dumb day to get married, but it was Travis's favorite holiday.

"Daddy said you and Travis been sweet on each other since third grade," Crickett said.

Faye laughed. "He used to pinch me when we took

the school boat into Bayou Bridge before the road was built."

"I would have hated him forever," Crickett declared. "Icky pinching boys."

"I used to," Faye admitted, reaching over to tickle Crickett. "But sometimes annoying boys turn into handsome fiancés."

The date of the wedding had been decided before Mamma's accident. At first, it was going to be at St. Paul's where everybody got married, but then Faye changed her mind. Since Mamma couldn't be carried into the church, Faye now wanted to get married at home.

Daddy had looked at her sideways, scratching the top of his ear. "I know your mamma wouldn't want to miss your special day, but she won't even know it's happening." Then he patted her shoulder. "We'll do the nicest wedding we can, bébé. You and Travis been planning a long time before Mamma's accident ever happened."

"Oh, Daddy." Faye had thrown her arms around his neck and burst into tears.

I couldn't figure out why Faye wanted to get married at all. How could she leave home and go live in Biloxi, Mississippi? The worst part of Faye getting married was that it meant I'd have to take care of Mamma, and I couldn't even *think* about that, let alone do it. Mamma just had to wake up before the wedding!

Swinging my legs, I started thinking about how I could get Mamma to wake up. Nurse Wade said she needed doctors, but the doctors had already said there was nothing else they could do for her, that we just had to wait until Mamma decided to wake up on her own.

The sun came out from behind the clouds, and my mind started working even faster. I'd heard about a folk healer who lived in the swamp. A *traiteur*. Some of the kids at school said she was old and ugly and could turn you into a toad—or worse, a cockroach, but they also said that sometimes the swamp witch could treat you like a doctor could.

I cleared my throat. "Do you remember Mamma rowing all the way out to the *traiteur*'s shack to get a cure for Crickett when she was sick with the croup?"

Crickett's eyes lit up. "Mamma saw a voodoo lady for me?"

"Not voodoo," I told her. "A *traiteur*," I added in my best French accent.

"Why'd she do that?"

"Because she loves you so much," Faye said, smiling as she nuzzled Crickett's neck.

I rolled my eyes, trying not to puke the peach ice cream Miss Beaumont had served us earlier at school and trying to keep the jealousy down in my belly.

If Mamma had gone into the swamps like that by herself, then she was braver than I ever thought — especially for a mamma who liked girlie pink dresses and painting flowers.

Daddy stepped onto the galerie, rubbing a hand on the back of his neck. "Crisis over. It's best we try not to feed Mamma real food. Gotta let that IV liquid going into her stomach do its job."

When I went inside the house again, Mamma looked the same as she had before the gagging episode. She was still lying on her bed as lifeless as a statue.

Daddy wiggled Mamma's fingers and turned her wrist. "We gotta keep moving her limbs. Doctors said she'll freeze up if we don't. Rosemary, bébé," he said, bending closer. "You gotta wake up and try to eat. You're skinnier than a matchstick."

His voice was scratchy with love and pain. I dug both thumbs into my eye sockets to stop the burning and then remembered that I had a temporary escape plan. "Daddy, could I spend the night at Jeannie's? She invited me."

He blinked. "Well, honey, I —"

Faye interrupted. "You are so selfish, Livie. Don't you have *any* feelings?"

"Will you sit here a spell?" Daddy suddenly asked her.

Faye took a step back, surprised. "'Course, Daddy."

Without another word, he walked out the back door and down to the dock. Three seconds later, I was running down the slope of lawn and folding myself onto the damp earth beside him. There were tears lying in the crevice of his leathery cheek, and seeing those tears seemed to take the life out of me. Fathers weren't supposed to get scared or cry. It made the world feel turned upside down. The pain in my stomach rose into my chest, and I was sure that the hole in my heart spilled a tiny drop of blood.

A mosquito skimmed the rippling surface of the water, darting in and out of the elephant ears like it had gone crazy. I think I knew how that mosquito felt. Going crazy was right where I was, too.

Daddy wiped the sweat off his face. "She's the air in my lungs," he said in a hoarse voice. "I can't seem to breathe right without her."

The air became thick as sugared molasses, turning dark, like the sun had suddenly disappeared. I couldn't seem to breathe right, either. I choked and began to cough.

Daddy picked me up off the bank. He swept the sticky strands of my hair back off my forehead with his rough fingers. "What's this, Sugar Bee?"

I loved how he called me that. Sounded like "shuh-guh" in his deep, throaty voice. I sucked in hot, moist air. The sun appeared again, coming out of the shadows behind the clouds.

"You breathing all right now?"

I nodded and laid my head against his shoulder.

"Don't do that, Livie girl. Holding your breath like that, turning blue."

"I—Mamma—" I tried to speak, but the words tangled up like socks in a dryer.

"Shh, now, don't say a word. There's no need. I know what you're thinking, Sugar Bee."

He was wrong. Daddy didn't know what I was thinking. If he knew, he'd hate me. I tried not to even look him in the eye anymore. His blue eyes could always read a person's soul. And my soul had gone south into wickedness. If Daddy asked me straight out what I was thinking, I'd probably end up lying—which would add another black deed to my list.

"You gotta have faith," he went on. "Me, I'm trying to. God knows I'm trying the best I can."

That was part of the trouble. I knew He was watching.

"Shoulda done something long ago," he choked out, as if talking to himself.

"Done what?"

Daddy shook his head. "Never you mind, Sugar Bee. Not yours to worry about."

Before I could ask again, a yellow taxicab with the words *New Orleans Number 235* swung past the oak trees. The car bumped over the pothole in the road, then bounced over the washboard driveway. The cab came to a halt in the empty spot next to Daddy's blue truck.

The driver laid a hand on the horn, giving several sharp blows.

I squinted at the people sitting in the backseat. "Who're they?"

Daddy said, "I believe the outside world has just arrived. It's your aunt Colleen and cousin Thibodaux."

Chapter 4

THE WORLD WAS CHANGING RIGHT AND LEFT.

"Hells bells, J.B., why'd you bring her home? She belongs in a hospital." Aunt Colleen finished tucking clean sheets around Mamma as I came into the house the next morning.

Daddy hunched over a steaming cup of coffee, sipping slowly. "They couldn't do nothin' more for her. She belongs at home with those that love her."

Aunt Colleen marched to the stove to attack a pot of grits with a spoon. "Are you implying I don't love her if I think a hospital is better?"

"Now, me, I didn't say that, Colleen," Daddy said, leaning back in his chair. "I know you wouldn't hike all the way down here from the north country if you didn't love her. And if anybody can help Rosemary, it's a nurse like you."

Aunt Colleen sniffed, as if glad to be appreciated.

"Come on over here, Livie and Crickett, and eat your breakfast before it gets cold."

"I was planning on sweeping out Mamma's art studio and washing the windows," I told her.

"Well, you need your energy to do all that work, so come fill up. Besides, we're tackling the house first before we do any other outside chores."

I couldn't help scowling inside. Seemed like Aunt Colleen was just going to be someone else to boss me around.

"How long you been a nurse, Aunt Colleen?" Crickett asked, climbing onto a chair stacked with phone books so she could reach the table.

"Thirty years. Got some experience with coma patients, too. We're going to get your Mamma well. She'll be up and talking in no time. You wait and see."

Crickett's eyes filled. "Oh, Aunt Colleen, really, truly?"

Aunt Colleen put her arms around Crickett and kissed the top of her head. "Don't you worry, sweetheart."

I stared at my hardening grits, wanting someone to call me sweetheart and kiss my hair. "How old are you, Aunt Colleen?" I asked. "Thirty years as a nurse is an awfully long time."

My aunt gave a humph, but smiled as though she liked the attention. "I'm fifty-three, and look every day of it, thank you very much."

I did the math in my head. That meant Aunt Colleen was eighteen years older than Mamma, although she was still younger than Daddy, who had turned fifty-five last month. I couldn't remember the last time Colleen had been here for a visit, but I'd seen snapshots tucked into Christmas cards. Mamma talked to Aunt Colleen on the telephone on the first day of every month like clockwork.

I added some butter to my bowl and studied my aunt. Colleen Allain Benoit was tall like Mamma, and even though it was warm in the kitchen, she'd tied a floppy hand-knitted pink sweater around her middle. Her hair was straight and she wore bangs, which I thought was strange. Most older ladies cut their hair real short and had it styled every week at the beauty parlor.

Aunt Colleen's hair was completely gray, too, like long strands of silver Christmas tree tinsel.

She took a scouring pad to the stove, and then held it up to inspect an inch of grease. Frowning at the sponge, she went on talking. "Your mamma's what's called a change-of-life baby. That's why I'm so much older than she is."

"What's a change-of-life baby?" Crickett asked.

The more Aunt Colleen scrubbed, the more she talked. "It means our parents were older. I think my mother was forty-five when Rosemary was born. I was in my first year of nursing school and my folks had a newborn. They called Rosemary their blessing. I thought she was adorable, but unfortunately, we never got a chance to be like real sisters growing up." She gave a quick glance into the front room where Faye and Daddy were checking Mamma's IV levels. "Until now," she added, her briskness changing to tenderness.

Faye came into the kitchen for a damp cloth. She reached over and squeezed Aunt Colleen, laying her head briefly on the woman's shoulder.

"Now what's that for?" Aunt Colleen said, laughing.

Faye lowered her voice, and I wished Crickett would stop kicking the table leg so I could hear better.

" —just so glad you're here," Faye said softly. "I didn't know what to do, I'm so tired."

"I know, honey, I know," Aunt Colleen said, putting a hand up to Faye's face.

A queer wave of envy swept over me. Since when was Faye all close and confiding with Aunt Colleen? Once again, I was pushed out of the circle, as if I didn't belong in my own family.

"Do you have other kids besides Thibodaux?" Crickett asked next. "I can't remember."

Aunt Colleen rinsed out the sponge. "That's because I haven't seen you since you were knee high to a grasshopper. Yep, I have two daughters. They're both married with a little one each. I'm a grandmother."

A grandmother! I'd never known anybody with grandchildren who was still raising kids as young as Thibodaux. He was younger than me!

Aunt Colleen's eyes crinkled and then she winked at me like we had a special secret. "I can see your brain whirring, Olivia. Yes, Thibodaux is *my* change-of-life baby. I did the same thing my mother did. Now that's a funny joke on me."

I picked up my bowl and stuck it in the sink, carefully rinsing and stacking it, something I'd never done before without my mamma asking me three times over. It felt strange, but good.

Aunt Colleen raised an eyebrow as she inspected the house. I could feel her grading the housekeeping from the last few weeks while Mamma was in the hospital. C+ for clutter. D- for kitchen scum. What grade would my aunt give us for how well we were taking care of Mamma? Faye got an A+, Crickett a second A for perfect shadowing, and me? I'd flunked out the very first night. I pictured Aunt Colleen smacking a big red F on the refrigerator with my name on it.

"How old is Thibodaux?" I already had a pretty good idea from looking him over the night before, but maybe if I kept asking questions, my aunt wouldn't spend so much time studying me.

"Turned nine last month." Aunt Colleen twisted around. "And speak of the darling devil, here he comes now. What a sleepyhead. Poor boy, we had to get up so early to get to the airport yesterday."

Thibodaux was still wearing his pajamas, red plaid with buttons and a pocket on the shirt. His wiry red hair stuck straight up as if it had been glued into place. He hadn't bothered to comb it or wash his face, either. Sleep crusted his eyes. Red freckles sprayed across his nose and even his lips were dotted with freckles, too. If I were him, I'd hate that.

Thibodaux stopped to stare at Mamma lying on the hospital bed. He'd stared the night before, too. Had he forgotten she was in a coma or did he just plain lose his manners every single time he saw my mother? I wanted to scream, "That's not really my mamma! In real life, she's beautiful!" 'Course, I didn't say a word, but I kept getting the urge to punch him.

"Do you call Thibodaux your blessing?" Crickett asked.

Aunt Colleen's face softened. "I sure do, honey."

Thibodaux scraped a chair across the floor, and Aunt Colleen set a plate of breakfast in front of him. He started wolfing down the food like he hadn't eaten in a week.

"What're you looking at?" Thibodaux barked at me.

I shrugged. I could understand why Daddy had called Aunt Colleen to come help nurse Mamma, but why did she have to bring this kid? He could have stayed home with his father, couldn't he?

Thibodaux stopped chewing to stare at me. I stared back, but my stomach jumped like a nervous cat. The house felt unstable, as if Thibodaux was purposely trying to make me mad.

"I'm going to call you T-Boy instead!" Crickett said excitedly. "Your real name is too hard to say every time I want to talk to you."

Thibodaux's head shot up. Pieces of egg clung to his lower lip. "That's a stupid name!"

Aunt Colleen pushed up her cardigan sleeves. "T-Boy means you've been welcomed into the family."

He gave her a grumpy look, and I could tell Thibodaux wasn't sure whether to believe his mother or not.

"Now all you kids get dressed so we can do the chores. This place looks like a cyclone blew through here. I can't begin to think with all the mess."

"Where'd Faye go?" Crickett asked.

Aunt Colleen nodded toward the porch where Faye sat holding the phone to her ear. The twisty telephone cord stretched all the way from the wall to the door. "Told me she was going to call some young man named Travis?"

"Travis is beautiful," Crickett said with a sigh.

Aunt Colleen laughed. "I guess that might account for something."

"He joined the navy," I said in his defense.

"And I hear they're getting married in a month!" Aunt Colleen exclaimed. "That girl's only seventeen."

"Mamma was barely eighteen when she married Daddy," I said.

"I can't deny that," my aunt said, handing me a wet, soapy cloth to wipe down the table.

I took the rag, wishing I could go outside to work for Mamma like I'd planned. I was sure the art cottage needed someone to clean it. Nobody had been out there in weeks and it had to be a mess. The best part was that if I cleaned the art cottage I would be doing something just for my mamma and her alone. And I'd get out of the house at the same time.

Aunt Colleen polished the juice glasses. "Girls down here still get married young, barely out of high school. I'm not used to that anymore, living up north."

"Do you like Montana?" I asked, crumbs flying to the floor as I swiped the rag across the Formica table.

"Beautiful big-sky country. Small towns like here. Peaceful, friendly folks, too."

"How could you leave your job for so long?"

"That part was easy. I haven't taken vacation in five years. Been saving all my days off—for what exactly, I couldn't tell you, but when your daddy called me up to tell me he'd brought Rosemary home, I told my supervisor that after thirty years with hardly a sick day I was going to stay as long as I need to."

"Don't T-Boy have a daddy?" Crickett asked.

Thibodaux pushed his chair back, almost knocking into the glass hutch. Mamma's wedding dishes gave a high-pitched tremor. He disappeared down the hall in ten seconds flat. What was that all about? I wondered.

"That's the sorrowful part of my life, little Crickett," Aunt Colleen said slowly. "My husband made a career out of the army and got back a year ago from the war. He's in the Veterans Hospital recuperating. Too much war sadness locked inside."

I swallowed hard. Mamma hadn't told me that story. Or maybe she had and I hadn't been listening too good. What would it be like to have your own daddy go crazy?

Crickett wiped at the tears slipping out of her eyes. "Will he ever get well again?"

"I hope so, honey. I sure hope so." Aunt Colleen handed Crickett a tissue to wipe her eyes. "Now don't go crying over him. He'll be all right one day." She gave a sad little laugh. "I just hope it's before Thibodaux's all grown up."

What was worse—a father in a hospital gone crazy from the war or your mother in a coma like she was dead? I shivered, thinking about Thibodaux's daddy having that sadness locked inside of him. Had he gone crazy because of some secret guilt he was hiding?

Faye came through the back door with a goofy smile on her face. She leaned against the stove next to Aunt Colleen, looking dreamy and completely silly. "Travis and me were talking wedding plans."

"I'm sure you have a lot to talk about, but at the moment the most important thing is getting this house back together. Then I'm going to teach you how to tend to your poor mother."

"What's wrong with the house?" I asked.

Aunt Colleen said a silent prayer to the ceiling. "For starters, there's enough old newspapers stacked around here to wallpaper the entire house twice with the front page. That'll be Thibodaux's assignment. Faye, you're on bathroom duty; Crickett, find the broom and sweep the porches. And Livie, I'd like your help in the kitchen."

My heart sank. I had already made a date with the broom, and now Crickett was skipping outside with it in her sweaty little hands. "Faye usually does kitchen stuff," I said, but my aunt didn't hear me. Or didn't want to.

Aunt Colleen clapped her hands. "First on the agenda, we'll scour the stove, then the walls, and then the floors."

"Why don't we just scrub the ceiling while we're at it?" I muttered.

Aunt Colleen started on the stove while I got a bucket of water and a scrub brush and began the floor. We worked in silence, and when I got to the doorway, I glanced up just in time to see Thibodaux poking at Mamma's legs with a rolled-up newspaper, as if she were a half-dead bug he was trying to get moving.

"Stop that!" I yelled.

Thibodaux jumped, and then stuck out his tongue.

I was so surprised, I didn't get a chance to return the favor.

Aunt Colleen called out, "Thibodaux, take those newspapers out to the front porch and tie them down so they don't blow away."

"Did you see what he did?" I asked.

"See what?"

"Poking Mamma's legs."

"Oh, I'm sure you didn't see right. He'd never do something like that."

"I ain't blind."

"Don't get impertinent with me, young lady."

I let out a gasp just as Thibodaux slammed the front door, leaving the house as fast as he could. I wanted to shake the freckles right off his red face.

I knew I shouldn't have said what I did, but Aunt Colleen was starting to make me mad. I was getting in trouble for something her son had done! And he was the one that stormed out of the house like a brat.

Aunt Colleen changed the subject. "How long has Crickett been like that?"

I pushed my rag across the dirty linoleum, not looking at her, feeling sulky. "Like what?"

"Weeping over every little thing. Did that start with your mother's accident?"

I felt the grits settle like heavy grease in my gut. Was she going to start asking questions about Mamma and the accident like Mrs. Guidry? "Nope," I managed to say. "It's just a personality trait."

"She's had a pretty short life to be crying so much."

"She's just tenderhearted. You should see her carry on when a june bug gets squished. She cried for a week when Sheila got run over."

Aunt Colleen sat back on her heels. "Good heavens! Who's Sheila?"

"Our hound dog."

"Oh." Relief spilled over Aunt Colleen's face. "For a second I thought you meant a member of the family I didn't know about."

"Sheila *was* a member of the family. And it only happened right before Mamma . . . so don't say nothing to Crickett about it and get her started again." I hadn't meant to lecture my own aunt. Daddy had always taught me to be respectful to grown-ups even if they asked too many questions.

"I guess Crickett's little body has a heart that's just too big for it."

"Guess so," I said softly, regretting how I'd shaken her off last night. Crickett was scared, too, and only five. I needed to be more patient.

I rinsed out the rags to tackle the corners. As I worked, I listened to Daddy talking to Mamma in the next room. He was speaking to her real slow and easy, and I wished I could be like him. I wished Mamma and me could love each other like that.

I was concentrating so hard I didn't notice that Aunt Colleen had stopped her own work to stare at me. "You've done that corner three times now, Livie."

"It's clean now, ain't it?" I said. Maybe if I worked harder, scrubbed until my fingers were raw, I could rub away all my bad deeds, too.

The next instant, Aunt Colleen crouched next to me. I almost stopped breathing. Aunt Colleen's silver hair hung like a curtain, tickling my arm. Her dark green eyes looked like gator eyes.

"That's a heavy load you're carrying, Olivia. Care to unload the burden?"

"I'm carrying nothing but an old, grungy rag." I held my breath, afraid of where the conversation was headed.

"I got eyes, don't I?" Aunt Colleen insisted. "I don't think I need a second pair to see that you're walking around with the most stooped shoulders I've ever seen on an eleven-year-old youngster."

"Nothing wrong with me," I said, lifting the bucket of dirty water.

"I think I'm more worried about you than all of Crickett's sentimental tears."

I was going to explode like a firecracker if I didn't get out of there. Why'd Aunt Colleen have to come all the way here from Montana and start poking around inside my head?

"Your mamma will get better, sweetie."

"What if she doesn't?" I cried, and the words felt like an explosion coming out of my mouth.

"Ever tried looking at the glass of milk half full instead of half empty?"

"My mamma's not a glass of milk!" I threw the rag across the room and then kicked the bucket with my foot. Dirty water raced across the floor like a dam had broken.

Aunt Colleen let out a screech as water poured over her brown loafers. She tried to stand, but slipped and fell bottomfirst. Her flowered dress mopped up the spilled greasy water like a thirsty sponge, then climbed up her bare legs. As water sloshed through the kitchen into the next room, Daddy ran over just in time to see Aunt Colleen with her feet over her head. His face had a look of pure terror, and then he let out a choked laugh.

"I didn't mean to!" I cried, but I couldn't look at my aunt. The sight of her was too embarrassing, and I couldn't look at my daddy, either. He'd think I was just pure wickedness.

The screen door cracked behind me like a gunshot as I raced across the lawn. When I got to the edge of the bayou, I jumped into my pirogue. Grabbing the pole, I clawed through the water with frantic, hard strokes. In two seconds, I was out of sight of the house.

Chapter 5

SWEAT STREAMED DOWN MY FACE, GETTING IN my mouth, running in my ears. I shouldn't have dumped that bucket and run out on Aunt Colleen, but she should mind her own business and not ask questions that don't have any answers.

Cupping my hands into the river, I splashed my face to cool off. I wished I could dump a bucket right over my whole head.

I couldn't go back home. Daddy would look at me with his sorrowful eyes, and I'd want to melt into the floor like a pound of butter on a hot July day.

Digging in my pole, I realized this was only the second time I'd been in my boat since Mamma's accident: yesterday with Daddy emptying the crawfish traps, and now. Jumping into the pirogue was one of those reflexes, like when the doctor tapped my knee with that little rubber mallet and my leg jolted forward all by itself.

My head shot up when I heard voices from the Landrys' fishing shack. All the Landry kids were outside hanging socks and shirts on the clothesline, mending nets, or running around creating a ruckus playing tag. I didn't feel like being friendly and wished I'd been paying more attention when my boat started floating in this direction.

A boy with dark hair and wearing a ball cap was swinging an ax as he cut a stack of firewood at the side of the house. He stopped chopping wood to watch me glide by. It was that T-Jacques Landry. "Halloo, Livie!" he called from the shore.

I laid the pole across my knees, looking straight ahead. T-Jacques showed up at the most peculiar times, whether it was following me around at the Broussards' fais do-do family dances on the weekends or popping up in front of me when I came around the corner at the Piggly Wiggly.

T-Jacques lifted his arms clear over his head and gave that piece of wood a huge wallop with his ax. The log cracked clean down the middle. When the two pieces rolled away, T-Jacques glanced up again. It occurred to me that he was showing off. Our eyes met and I felt my stomach jump. T-Jacques smiled broadly, as if he was pleased to know I'd looked in his direction.

I hadn't seen him since he moved up to seventh grade this past year. We'd never been in the same class before, but I used to see him during lunch, running with the other boys or playing softball. When I'd head for the swings, T-Jacques always glanced in my direction and smiled.

I frowned, wondering why my gut leaped every time I saw him. It made me mad that he had that effect on me. Like I was almost excited to see him looking at me. I sure didn't want some boy thinking I was pleased to see him. Even if he did have nice eyes.

I could just blame it on Aunt Colleen's grits. They *had* been lumpy that morning.

Turning the pirogue around, I poled back toward my own house against the current, keeping my face forward. From the corner of my eye, I could see T-Jacques still gazing at me like a dope. I focused on keeping my own stupid smile from lifting the corners of my mouth.

"'Bye, Livie!" he called, but I managed not to turn around.

Within minutes, the Landry place was gone and the thicket of cypress trees near my own yard closed around me as I poled through. The sprawling giant oaks and tall, straight cypresses gathered me inside like a mother hen hugging her chicks. Nudging the boat forward, I liked to imagine I was in the middle of my own private forest.

Purple flowering water hyacinth spread across the sunlit surface like a quilt. Cypress knees jutted up near the banks, and I realized that I could spy on my own house without anybody seeing me. Thibodaux was digging in the dirt and Crickett crouched beside him, her baby-fine hair falling across her face like a shadow.

Reaching down, I plucked a few stems of the tiny purple flower to take back home. I could put them in a mason jar and set it on the table near Mamma's hospital bed.

I didn't know what I'd say to Aunt Colleen when I returned. She and Daddy were probably furious. I counted up my sins. Spilling the water bucket, drowning Aunt Colleen, not staying to clean up the mess. Oh, yeah, and being rude to grown-ups. They should all hate me. There were lots of reasons; these were only the latest.

I felt tears coming on and lay down in the bottom of the pirogue, crossing my arms and staring up through the branches. Crickets and cicadas buzzed in my ears. I was so tired I closed my eyes and decided to see if I could shut down all my body systems.

Miss Beaumont had taught us about systems. There was the circulatory, the skeletal, the digestive, and the muscular system. There were supposed to be five, but I couldn't remember the last one.

A moment later, I felt a sting as a mosquito bit my arm, and I slapped at it. Nervous system! The one that was connected to your brain. The system that made a person talk and laugh and smile, that made you *alive*.

Mamma's nervous system had shut down, as if someone had taken a pair of scissors and cut the wires to her brain. I wondered if she was aware of any sounds or voices. Could she see light behind her eyelids? I had no idea and neither did all the grown-ups, which seemed crazy. What were doctors *for* if they didn't know this stuff? They were supposed to *know.* Tears itched at my eyes, just as something bumped at the bottom of the boat.

I sat up with a start, gulping in hot, humid air. It was probably that scrunched-up-faced, big-old-forehead kid Thibodaux throwing rocks.

The bump came again, stronger. That wasn't no rock.

I peered over the edge, studying the murky water. A baby alligator skimmed just below the surface of the lily pads, yellow stripes like bright sunny rings around his body. He wasn't more than twelve inches long and newly hatched. As I watched, the baby gator raised his head and his black, beady eyes studied me right back.

What was an alligator doing here? Our cove was usually safe from alligators. We'd seen nests in the next bayou over, but not here. Maybe this one got separated from his mamma. At least I hoped so. I darted a glance around. There wasn't any sign of a big mamma gator, thank goodness, or I'd be poling as fast as I could for the pier and screaming bloody murder. A big mamma gator protecting her baby could tip me and the pirogue right over.

"Come here and let me take a look at you," I called softly.

The alligator dove down again and circled my boat. I waited for the right moment. When he paused on his third loop, I scooped both my hands fast as I could through the top of the water and caught him, holding him close so he wouldn't squirm between my fingers and get away. He thrashed like a wild thing, but I quickly set him down between my feet. He crawled along the boat's bottom ridge, and I reached out a hand to touch his jagged back. My heart swelled inside my chest. "I done caught you all by myself!"

My daddy had caught baby alligators lots of times during hatching season. He'd scoop one up in his net and then let me run my fingers down his back before releasing the gator back into the water.

"They's cute and tempting to turn 'em into a pet, Sugar Bee, but it's not a good idea," he'd always say, giving me his warning lecture. "Alligators ain't puppies or kittens. Gators get dangerous when they get used to people. Seen it more than once—a gator come looking for food and bite someone's hand off. You leave 'em in the wild where they belong."

Daddy's words hummed in my head as I stroked the baby alligator. He calmed down easy as pie. He was so small, and so cute, I couldn't help loving him instantly. He scurried along the ridge of the pirogue's hull, and then stopped to open his mouth, showing off a set of tiny, razor-sharp teeth.

"Don't threaten me, you naughty thing. You can't bump my boat and not let me hold you."

I maneuvered the pirogue out of the cove and drifted along the patch of elephant ears. When I glanced up, Jeannie's face was looking at me from the bow of her skiff. "Hey, where'd you come from?" I cried.

"Thought I'd paddle down the bayou and see what I could see," my friend said. "And you got yourself a baby gator!"

I nodded. "Isn't he beautiful?"

Jeannie leaned over to touch the top of his head. "I think he likes you."

I held him up and looked him in the eye. He opened his mouth and showed off his tiny pearly teeth. "I think I'll call you T-Baby." The tiny gator was staring up at me as if I was his mamma. It was the funniest thing.

"What are you gonna do with him? You aren't taking him home, are you?"

I shrugged. "No, just keeping my eye on him."

"My daddy would tan my hide if he saw me with a baby alligator."

"My daddy, too," I admitted, but a longing rose in my heart. I wanted that baby gator to be mine. Besides, he wouldn't get more than a couple of feet long for more than a year. Reluctantly, I held him over the boat's edge to let him crawl off my palms and glide back into the water. He disappeared under an elephant ear, and

I could see him peeking at me as if daring me to grab him again.

"You can go for now," I told him, like a toddler. "But don't get into no trouble."

"Whatcha doin'?" A voice asked off to my right.

I squinted into the sun. Crickett and Thibodaux stood on the bank staring at me with mouths open. My few minutes of a peaceful mood shattered. "None of your business," I said.

It gave me a start, wondering how long they'd been there watching me. I hoped they hadn't seen the alligator. I looped the rope of the pirogue around the dock piling and made a quick bowline knot. Jeannie tied up her own boat and jumped onto the lawn.

"You put something into the water," Thibodaux said.

So they *had* been spying on me! I was going to have to be careful.

"Who are you?" my cousin added, looking at Jeannie.

Jeannie flicked the tail of her cornrow braid over her shoulder. "I'm Jeannie, Livie's best friend."

"He's our cousin Thibodaux," Crickett said. "From Montana."

I laid my pole in the bottom of the pirogue so it wouldn't float off, not looking at my cousin, hoping I could brush him off like a bothersome fly.

"What'd you put in the water just now?" Thibodaux asked again.

I motioned for Jeannie to follow me up to the house. "That's for me to know—and you to find out."

"I'll tell my mamma on you."

"So tell her. See if I care. Come on, Jeannie."

I stomped through the back door, wanting to grumble about the annoying little kids, but I knew I didn't have any right to complain after running off. I was afraid I was going to get yelled at or grounded from Jeannie's house forever.

Daddy was nowhere in sight. The kitchen was empty. Only Faye was around, finishing Mamma's makeup.

"Come see, Livie," Faye called. "I put some new colors on Mamma."

I hung in the doorway, goose bumps rising on my skin. I held my breath as Jeannie stepped forward, her mouth open. My palms got sweaty and my heart thudded in my throat. It was the first time Jeannie had seen my mother since the accident. I was afraid she might run away screaming.

Mamma moved her legs restlessly under the sheets. Her mouth hung slack, eyes half open. I could never figure out if she was asleep or getting ready to die right then and there. My stomach felt like it was in my throat all the time.

Aunt Colleen came down the hall and entered the living room. She'd changed out of her wet dress and put on a cotton shift as well as dry sandals. She stared at Faye's makeup job. "What in the world are you doing?"

"I—I'm not doing anything—" Faye started.

Aunt Colleen drew closer, a frown wrinkling her face. "It's not bad enough that you put your mother in the front room where the neighbors can see her. Now you have to paint her up like she's a doll!"

"I'm not trying to paint her," Faye tried to explain. "Just make her pretty. Like she did every morning."

"Your mother is not a toy. She's a very sick woman."

"Daddy says if Mamma's in the front room she'll get to see us when she wakes up," I said. "Maybe she can even hear us while she's sleeping so she doesn't feel lonely."

Aunt Colleen sighed as though we were trying her patience. "I don't want to scare you girls, but people in comas do not feel lonely. They are not sleeping. And they do *not* care if they are wearing makeup."

I wondered how Aunt Colleen knew Mamma wasn't just sleeping. Did she know for sure that Mamma couldn't hear us talking? Mamma's ears hadn't suddenly stopped working, had they?

"And I'm absolutely certain," Aunt Colleen added evenly, "your mother would be mortified if she knew that every person who walked into this house could see her lying there wearing only a nightgown."

Faye bit her lips. "I've never let anyone but family see Mamma in her nightgown."

Aunt Colleen stared around the room, first at Mamma, then at Faye, and finally settling on me. "It appears to me Livie's inviting the neighborhood in."

Jeannie put her head down and backed toward the door.

I swallowed. "That's my best friend, Aunt Colleen."

"It's not a good time for playing with friends, Olivia. Your timing is very thoughtless. That goes for most of the things I've seen you do, and I've only been here one day."

I knew I should apologize right then or I'd lose Jeannie's company for the rest of the day, but I couldn't bring up the words. They were shoved too far down my throat. Besides, I didn't want to do it in front of everybody, like I was onstage and they were the audience.

Then I wondered if I had to apologize at all. Didn't seem like Aunt Colleen approved of anything I did. And I hated her calling me Olivia. I'd told her when she arrived that I never went by that name, but she had a short memory. Or maybe she was just trying to get under my skin. I didn't think she was being too nice to Faye, either.

My urge to stick up for my older sister surprised me. What was the harm in a little makeup?

Faye's face was red and splotchy as she returned the makeup bottles to the box. She arranged each lip color in a row, screwed on the powder jar lid, and then snapped the compact shut. "Just thought doing Mamma's makeup was something normal in a world that's turned inside out wrong."

Before Aunt Colleen could say anything else, Crickett banged through the screen door. "I figured out how to cure Mamma," she announced.

"And what's that?" Aunt Colleen asked.

"Take her to the voodoo priestess!"

"Good heavens, child, what are you talking about?"

Faye set down the makeup box and pulled Crickett close. "I think she means the *traiteur* that lives in the swamp a couple miles from here, Aunt Colleen."

"Surely people don't believe in that nonsense anymore!"

"The Landry kids say she lives with a house full of rats so smart they hold conversations every night at the supper table," Crickett said, her eyes growing big.

Faye laughed and I found myself holding back a giggle, too.

Jeannie let out a snort. "Buddy Avery once said that if you make the *traiteur* angry she'll curse you with a rash that makes you itch so bad your skin will fall clean off your body."

"Let's stop this talk right now," Aunt Colleen ordered. "*Traiteurs* are supposed to be healers, and they do not work hoodoo magic or stare into crystal balls like those voodoo priestesses in New Orleans. Even so, they can't cure diseases and they most certainly can't cure a coma. That's a lot of rubbish." Aunt Colleen's words had a tone of finality, but I couldn't stop thinking about it.

Daddy had always forbidden us to take the boat beyond our own bayou, so I'd never seen the *traiteur*. Seems like I'd heard her name once, but I couldn't remember what it was. Only that she was supposed to be about a hundred years old. There were strange stories, but good stories floated around, too. Rumors that *traiteurs* lived like regular folks and paid house calls to give you herbs or pray over you.

As if reading my mind, Jeannie spoke up. "I met a *traiteur* once."

Aunt Colleen raised her eyebrows. "Is that so?"

"Last summer when we were in Houma visiting my cousins, everybody starting getting warts. Loads of 'em. My parents were gone on a fishing trip and we stayed a whole month. My aunt got a *traiteur* to come and cure all us kids. She rubbed a potato on our warts."

Crickett giggled. "A potato? Like the ones you mash and put gravy on?"

"Yep. We had to bury the potato under the porch of the house where the rain falls. The *traiteur* said that as soon as the potato rotted in the ground, the warts would be gone — poof!"

"I remember that!" I said. "You had warts on both your pinkie fingers and they disappeared when you got back. I saw it with my own two eyes." I darted a quick glance at Mamma. I wished I could ask her if the *traiteur*'s herbs had worked for Crickett when she had the croup. They must have. I couldn't recall Mamma ever taking Crickett to the doctor.

Aunt Colleen lifted Mamma's hand and ran her fingers down her arm. My mother never stirred. If I was asleep and someone grabbed my arm, I'd jump through the roof, scream bloody heck, or throw a pillow at them.

Mamma didn't do a darn thing. She didn't even twitch, like her soul had already left her body and she was just an empty shell lying on that hospital bed.

My mind kept working on the idea of that old woman healer in the swamp. Maybe she didn't practice hoodoo magic or stick pins into voodoo dolls as the kids at school liked to say. Maybe she was a real *traiteur*—someone who could heal.

Chapter 6

THE *TRAITEUR* WAS STILL ON MY MIND THE NEXT
morning when I stood at the bathroom mirror with the
scissors and a hunk of hair in my fist. Just a trim to help
it lay flat. Mamma had been after me to do something
with my hair to keep it from flying around like cotton
candy—and to stop wearing pigtails! After all, she'd
said, I'd be a teenager next year. Like I didn't know my
own birthday.

I was focusing so hard on keeping my wet hair
straight so I could snip off the last inch that sweat was
dribbling down my upper lip. I licked off the salt and
rubbed my hand across my mouth. This was harder than
I thought. The mirror even steamed up.

Crickett banged on the door. "I need to use the
bathroom!"

"Go away!" I shouted, but I was nearly finished.

I twisted around to see how the back came out. My
hair was crooked right in the middle, dipping like an

uneven smile. Oh, well. Maybe Faye would help me. If I asked real nice. And said please. And did her dishes for a week.

I ran my fingers through my damp hair. Maybe the uneven edge wouldn't be so noticeable once it started to dry—and if I put a ribbon in it. Hey, there was a good idea!

I rummaged in the bottom drawer where all the hair stuff was kept and found dozens of pink and red ribbons, all different lengths and widths. Yuck. Not my colors at all, but I kept digging, and at the bottom I finally found a deep-sea-green ribbon. That would look nice but not too girly. I tied it around my hairline, letting the edges of the ribbon flutter past my ears. Okay, not too bad.

Catching my reflection, I noticed that I was rolling my eyes. Then I stared harder, leaning against the bathroom counter until my thighs hurt.

Trimming my hair up and putting in a ribbon made me look different, older. I gave a gulp and touched the ends of my hair. I had to admit I kind of liked it. I looked like one of the girls at school instead of a little kid. Almost *pretty*, like Mamma. That didn't seem possible, even though it would be nice to be pretty like my mamma was, and I'd sometimes wondered if I ever would be.

I put away the scissors, the hairbrush, and the bits of ribbons, and narrowed my eyes. So now, I had to decide if I wanted to look like a regular girl. My daddy liked me just as I was. I was usually so busy helping him that I didn't have time to worry about what I wore or how I looked. I always fought Mamma's efforts to clean me up, curl my hair, or change into something besides jeans and stained work shirts. I figured she wanted to make me into Faye, but maybe I needed to think about it some more. At the moment, I couldn't make too many changes at once. And I was still light-years behind Faye in the female department. Which was fine with me.

Cautiously, I opened the bathroom door, peeked out, then headed through the front door, planning to go around the side of the house to the backyard and hoping I didn't see anybody along the way.

Instead, I ran smack into Miss Beaumont on the porch. She was wearing a linen dress and heels. A white handbag hung off her arm all proper-looking, but her hands were filled with an aluminum-wrapped plate. "Why, hello, Livie! I was hoping I'd see you. And hoping I could visit your mamma."

I had a huge temptation to throw the ribbon on the ground, stomp on it, and mess up my hair-brushing job, but that would only call attention to it, and I figured if I ignored it, everybody else might, too. I crossed my fingers behind my back just in case.

"Well, Mamma ain't exactly seeing visitors. She can't talk, you know."

Miss Beaumont's eyes crinkled. "I realize that, dear. Just wanted to drop off this batch of cookies, although I'm afraid I ended up eating more than I placed on the plate! I decided it was time to give some away or I'd soon be bigger than a hot air balloon."

"Thank you." I peeked under the aluminum foil. The smell of warm snickerdoodles hit my nose with a

96

wham. And every single one had lots of sugar in the middle, just like Mamma used to make them.

After a moment, Miss Beaumont gave a little laugh. "May I come in, Livie?"

"Oh, sure, I guess." Cautiously, I opened the front door and stepped inside, spying out the house. At least Mamma wasn't in her nightgown any longer. Aunt Colleen had dressed her in a cotton sundress today.

Aunt Colleen came forward as Miss Beaumont extended her hand. "Claire Beaumont. Livie's teacher at school."

"Pleased to meet you."

"How y'all doing?" Miss Beaumont said brightly.

There was a moment of silence while my aunt stopped talking to stare at my haircut and the green ribbon flopping in my eyes. "What did you do to your hair?"

I stared back, wishing she'd quit talking. "Nothing."

"I like it," Miss Beaumont said, reaching out to smooth the ribbon back in place. Her fingers were cool and soft on my cheek. Suddenly, emotion tugged at my eyes, and I bit my lip to stop the tears. I wished my mamma was awake to touch me like that. Stroke my face as if she liked me, and my haircut.

"Miss Beaumont brought us cookies," I said, clearing my throat and holding out the plate. "I'll take them to the kitchen."

"Thank you, Olivia," Aunt Colleen said.

I tried not to grimace as I passed through the front room and set the snickerdoodles on the kitchen table. Slipping two of the cookies into my palm, I dashed through the galerie and down the steps into the backyard.

At the edge of the bank, Daddy was bent over studying the muddy water. Dark stains of perspiration soaked his shirt. The afternoon was hotter than heck, the heat so thick I could practically mold it with my fingers.

I chewed the last of my second cookie and before I could blink again, Daddy started wading into the bayou. With his shoes and overalls on! He kept going, heading for the old cypress tree stump that sat off the shore.

That stump had been there since long before I was born or even before my Paw Paw was a baby. Daddy figured it was two hundred years old. The tree had been cut down during the old logging days, and Daddy said that when he was a boy he'd stand on the stump and use it like a diving board, but he wouldn't allow me or my sisters to dive off it. Said it was too shallow, even though during flood season, the water got more than ten feet deep and the stump disappeared.

I watched him circling the stump, waist deep in the water. The flat sawed-off surface peeped above the water-line. The rest of the tree's base was far below; its roots buried deep in the mud.

Daddy kicked at the stump, causing the water to ripple. I was surprised to see the old stump rock ever so slightly. It wasn't as solid as it appeared. The silt on the river's bottom must be shifting.

Next, Daddy wrapped his arms around it and pulled, trying to jiggle it loose like a rotten tooth. I knew he was strong, but nobody could pull a tree stump out of the water like that.

Daddy finally backed off and splashed water on his red face. His chest heaved as he dragged himself onto the dock again. Striding past the house, he disappeared around the side yard.

A second later, I jumped down the porch steps just as the blue Chevy barreled down the side yard toward the bank. Daddy slowed, then inched the truck to the water's edge. Thibodaux jumped out of the passenger side and stood on the dock, waving his hands to direct the vehicle's descent.

T-Boy yelled, "Stop!" and Daddy braked the truck.

Leaving the engine idling, Daddy and T-Boy consulted together, heads close. Daddy clapped a hand on T-Boy's shoulder and gave him a big one-armed hug. T-Boy was grinning like crazy.

Jealousy raced through my veins like poison. I wanted to be the one down there. If there was something to be accomplished, Daddy usually called for me.

I squirmed, thinking about the fact that just a few days ago, being invisible was just what I'd wanted. I guess God was giving me my wish, but now I wanted to change my mind.

A pile of rope came out of the back of the truck as I climbed onto the porch railing, legs dangling, my head buzzing with questions. As Daddy went back into the water, he lowered himself so that he was sitting neck-deep in the river. The rope went down with him, but I couldn't tell what he was doing. T-Boy kept directing as if he was some kind of expert.

Crickett ran down to the bank from where she'd been playing in the sandbox, talking and pointing alongside T-Boy. I bit my lip. What did those little kids know about anything?

Daddy strung the rope around the tree stump, knotting it good and tight. He backed off, and then tugged hard to test it. The rope stayed firm and taut, not loose.

When he waded out of the bayou, his boots squirted water with every step. He took the other end of the rope and secured it on to the truck's hitch, looping and knotting like he'd done with the stump. When he was finished, he climbed behind the wheel even though his clothes were drenched.

"Stay back now," he called out the window. "Don't know what that stump's gonna do when it comes jumpin' out of the mud. Keep to the dock out of the way."

"Yes, sir!" T-Boy shouted back.

I rolled my eyes, waiting for Thibodaux to give a military salute.

Daddy revved the engine, put it in gear, and then inched the truck up the lawn. The rope line went as taut as Paw Paw's fiddle string. Daddy kept the truck moving forward, one eye on the stump in the rearview mirror.

The rope strained and began to twist. Any second, I expected it to snap right in two. Black smoke spewed out the truck's tailpipe. Just when it looked like the rope would break, the cypress stump began to rock.

Crickett clapped her hands. "There it goes, Daddy!"

Thibodaux surveyed the situation. "I think you might be right, Crickett," he pronounced.

I rolled my eyes again and folded my arms across my chest, but nobody was paying me any attention.

Aunt Colleen came around the opposite side of the house followed by Miss Beaumont. My aunt had a basket of cucumbers and tomatoes in her hands. She set the vegetables down, shading her eyes with one hand.

"What're they trying to do?" Aunt Colleen asked. She didn't speak directly to me, but Faye was still inside the house with Mamma and I was the only one nearby.

My heart gave a lurch. Aunt Colleen's profile, the way she wiggled her fingers across her eyebrows to block the sun, was just like Mamma. I knew I should have already apologized to Aunt Colleen, but the words and the opportunity never seemed to come at the same time, even though I'd rehearsed them in my mind ten times the night before.

"Getting that tree stump outta there," I said. Actually, I was grateful my aunt wasn't a yeller like some mammas. That would be worse.

Miss Beaumont smiled as if she felt no tension at all. "I declare, this is the most excitement I've seen in ages."

"Things are pretty peculiar around here," Aunt Colleen said.

"When did you arrive?" Miss Beaumont asked.

"A few days ago."

Aunt Colleen looked at me when she said that. I knew my father wouldn't be happy if he knew I hadn't apologized. Maybe he did know. Was that why he hadn't invited me to help him with the stump? I stepped off the porch and sidled closer to my aunt, clearing my throat and feeling a burn of embarrassment all the way down to my stomach. I just had to get it over with.

"I—I'm sorry about yesterday, Aunt Colleen," I said, my voice coming out like a whisper about to vanish. "The water, I mean. I didn't mean to ruin your dress or hurt you."

Aunt Colleen studied my face, then nodded as though accepting my apology. Slowly, she said, "Just wish you'd spilled more than that bucket of water, Livie."

She'd called me Livie. Finally. I stared down at the slats of the porch, but thankfully, the roar of the truck filled up the emptiness. Miss Beaumont acted like she hadn't heard a thing. I felt a surge of love for my teacher even as she kept her eyes fixed on the truck's tires kicking up mud and grass.

"Think it'll work?" Aunt Colleen asked, her eyes lifting to the scene at the dock.

I gave a shrug. "Dunno, but Daddy usually knows what he's doing."

Something started groaning; the rope, the truck, the stump. Maybe all three. The groaning turned to an ear-splitting whine. The tires slipped on the dewy grass, and Daddy gunned the truck. That's when the rope began to unravel and the first thread snapped.

Miss Beaumont gave a screech and put a hand to her mouth.

Aunt Colleen started forward. "That rope is going to rip apart and send the truck careening down the lawn."

The next instant, the water churned with a monstrous whooshing roar as the old cypress stump popped out of the mud and fell over with a moan onto its side. Water shot sky-high, soaking Crickett and T-Boy standing on the dock. They started running around laughing at each other as the spray sparkled in the sunlight.

I could hear Daddy's whoop from inside the truck's cab. Setting the engine brake, he jumped out, running down to have a look at the upended tree stump.

"Guess it worked after all," Aunt Colleen said, shaking her head. "But sometimes this household makes no sense to me." She picked up the basket of vegetables. "Let me give you some of these fresh vegetables, Claire," she added to Miss Beaumont.

"Why, thank you, I'd be delighted. Let me help you."

Leaving my aunt and teacher, I slipped off the porch railing and ran down to the water's edge.

Up close, the tree stump was a monstrous swamp creature. Gnarly black roots dripping with gooey, green swamp moss, stuck up in the air like claws.

Daddy stuck his hands on his hips and hollered, "Worked, Livie!"

I couldn't help smiling back. "Yep, it sure did."

My daddy hadn't been this cheerful in weeks, and I felt a little ping of pleasure in my chest. I wanted to run to him and put my arms around his middle and squeeze, but he was too busy dancing around that stump with Thibodaux and Crickett. I couldn't bring myself to share in their joyful exhilaration watching that old stump get sucked right out of the bayou.

I wasn't sure I belonged to my own family anymore. And I certainly didn't deserve to dance and shout and be happy. I was also afraid that my daddy would be able to read my thoughts, that he'd look at my eyes and just know. So I was avoiding being too close.

How would he feel if he knew the truth — if he knew the real story of the past month?

How long could I stay submerged under my own layer of mud and silt before the truth reared its black, ugly claws and exposed me?

Chapter 7

"T-BOY AND I SAW YOU," CRICKETT WHISPERED
as I was trying to go to sleep the next night. Just outside
the door to the galerie, I heard the porch light sizzle as a
gnat flew into the bulb and got fried.

"Don't know what you're talking about," I said, rolling
on to my back as every fiber of my being went on high
alert. Had my little sister seen me in the bayou with
Mamma? Were there *witnesses* to my crime? My pillow was
on fire, the room hotter than a frog on a roasting spit, even
with all the screens. June was turning into a heat wave.

"We saw you with that alligator," Crickett added.

I let out a sigh of relief so fast I swallowed wrong and
had to cough. Of course, they didn't see the accident.
T-Boy wasn't even here yet. Breathing normally again, I
said, "Is that right, Miss Snoopy?" So they *had* seen me
with my alligator, the little snitches.

"T-Boy knows about you."

I snorted. "He don't know nothing!"

Crickett's hair tickled my arm. "He says you must have a secret about Mamma since you won't never touch her."

"Thibodaux Benoit will be the *last* person to ever know anything about my true thoughts," I said indignantly, even as a feeling of alarm raced through me. What did my cousin suspect?

"He's cute," Crickett went on.

I almost gagged. "Who's cute — T-Boy?"

Crickett giggled. "No, that little gator. I want to pet him. Will you let me?"

I didn't answer right away. I knew that letting her go with me into the bayou to pet an alligator would get me into trouble for sure. The rule was that we had to be with a parent until we were eleven, and then only if we could aim and shoot a twenty-two. That was pretty much the law for every kid I knew.

"Maybe," I finally said. "If you don't mind only having eight or nine fingers."

Crickett laughed, knowing I was teasing her, and bounced on the bed. "Does he like chicken?"

"He's too little yet for that. He mostly eats bugs." I thought about how I'd sneaked away that morning before anybody else was awake and found T-Baby swimming under the elephant ears. I spent a half hour petting and talking to him, relieved that he hadn't swum away and gotten lost, or that his mamma hadn't swooped in and scurried him back to the nest.

I reached over and tickled Crickett's stomach to get her to stop talking about the baby gator. I didn't want her spilling the beans to Daddy or Aunt Colleen. She let out a shriek, then rolled over and returned the favor. Her chubby fingers were hot and sticky, but she got me in my neck and toes and even under my arms. I hated getting tickled; it made me want to pee my pants every time.

"Stop, I give up!" I finally snorted.

Crickett got the hiccups, and her hiccups sounded so hilarious I started giggling again. The kitchen light snapped on through the galerie door that led inside to the house, and I blinked in the sudden, bright light.

Aunt Colleen stood in the doorway wearing a bathrobe. "I'm sleeping by your mamma tonight. That means I'd like to *sleep* a little."

Crickett got on her knees, pulling her nightgown over her legs. "We're sorry, Aunt Colleen. We'll be quiet."

"Morning comes much too fast. Now you girls go to sleep, hear?" She turned, and then paused. "You okay, Livie?"

I jumped when I heard my name. "Yes, ma'am."

There was a moment of silence while Aunt Colleen seemed to be thinking. I dreaded her next words, but all she said was, "Well, then, good night."

The light snapped off and everything went dark. Even the outside porch light was off now, and the bugs stopped sizzling.

Crickett's toes tickled mine, and her breath was steamy and sweet, like Mamma's favorite perfume. "One of these days, Livie, you gotta talk to Mamma," she said in a drowsy voice. "Maybe Mamma misses you. Maybe she's just waiting for you to give her a hug."

An instant later Crickett was curled in a ball and asleep. I lay there, pinching back tears as my sister's words echoed inside my head. I was the last person Mamma would ever want to hug her or talk to her. Not after what I'd done.

Then I tried to remember the last time I'd hugged my mother. It was harder than I thought, but I finally figured it had to be the day Mamma had taken me shopping for an Easter dress in New Iberia.

Mamma wanted me to wear my dress shoes, which always gave me instant blisters. "Why can't I wear my sandals?" I'd asked as we drove off in Daddy's truck.

"It'll be easier to tell how the dress will look if you're wearing the right shoes," Mamma had said. One hand hung out her open window; sunglasses perched on her nose. She looked pretty in her sleeveless pink dress with the scooped neck and her cross on its gold chain lying against her skin. "Hmm. Yellow or blue? I'm thinking a yellow dress would look real nice with your hair."

"I don't want any new dress."

Mamma didn't seem bothered. "Will you let me brush out your hair real pretty for Sunday?"

I stared at the fields of sugarcane whizzing by.

"I like to go to church on Easter Sunday," Mamma went on, as if trying to keep the conversation going. "We don't go to Mass very often, but Easter Sunday we can all dress up. It'll be fun."

"Fun for Faye and Crickett."

Mamma sighed. "At least try, okay, Livie? Please?"

Even with her begging me all polite and pretty, all I could think about was how shopping made me miss a Saturday of fishing with Daddy.

Before we even left that morning, Mamma had put her foot down. "I won't have my daughter going to church in shorts. You're going to look like a young lady if it kills me."

"It's going to kill *me*!" I'd shouted back, which made my daddy take me aside for a talk.

"You don't have to like it," he said. "But do it for your mamma."

"Even if I go shopping with her, I still don't think she'll like me."

"You know that ain't true, Livie."

"She loves Faye and Crickett more," I'd grumbled. "I know it."

I remember Daddy sitting back, not speaking, and I was afraid it *was* true—that my mamma really did love my sisters best. Then he stroked his chin and said, "Your sisters might be easier for your mamma to love, but only because they like to do the same things and talk about the same subjects, but Crickett and Faye don't have a monopoly on your mamma's love. There's enough to go around for everybody."

"But they get it all and leave me with nothing!" I'd said, and was horrified when my voice started to shake like I was about to cry.

Daddy put his arm around me. "Livie, maybe your mamma has to work harder to understand you, but you have to work harder, too. When you *both* can accept each other no matter your differences, you'll have a love that's stronger and deeper than you thought possible.

Sometime love is a two-way bayou, and you, Sugar Bee, have to stop paddling away downstream."

I didn't understand everything he was trying to tell me, but he knew how to get me every time.

"Heck, Sugar Bee," he added. "Just for today, go shopping with your mamma. Do it for me if that makes you more willing."

So there I was, stuck in the hot car, driving farther away with every passing second.

Mamma gave up talking, but after we got to the dress shop, she seemed to perk up again. Hours seemed to go by as I threw a hundred dresses over my head. Mamma inspected each dress, along with an ambush of salesclerks with perpetual frowns and fake penciled eyebrows. They pulled at my arms or made me turn around until I was dizzy. Dresses of all different colors turned up in that dressing room, with lace, ribbons, buttons, you name it.

Mamma finally settled on one that wasn't too long or too short, too tight or too loose.

I'd never suffered so much in my entire life.

Afterward, Mamma treated me to lunch and that helped me feel a teensy bit better. Mamma even let me order an ice-cream sundae for dessert. The strawberries dripping over the cold ice cream were sweet and juicy, and I saved the cherry to eat last.

"While we're here, I'd like to take you by that historic plantation house, Shadows-on-the-Teche. You'll love it."

"We're not going home?" I'd thought lunch was the last stop and I'd be back in my shorts in an hour. "I don't want to see some stupid house."

"Give it a try, Livie. How you ever gonna expand your world? There's a whole lot more than pirogues and crawfish out there."

"What if I don't care about anything else?"

Mamma sighed again. She seemed to do that all the time, as if I was a thorn stuck in her big toe.

"I told you to leave me home. You should have brought Faye and Crickett."

"Maybe I should have!" Mamma snapped. Then she shook her head. "No, I didn't mean that. I've been wanting to spend time with you, Livie, and that's what we're doing. Even if it's hard on both of us."

I watched as she tried to laugh, but it came out sounding funny, like she wasn't sure she really meant it. Then Mamma put an arm around my shoulders and I returned the embrace, but only briefly, before running down the sidewalk. I figured the sooner we got the boring tour over with, the sooner we'd be home.

Shadows-on-the-Teche was pretty—if you liked old mansion houses with people dressed up, pretending they lived a hundred years ago. This one was built before the Civil War, the tour guide told us in a high, sugary voice. I counted eight enormous white columns strung across the wide porch, which were pretty stunning—if you liked mammoth white columns.

Inside, it was mostly old-fashioned furniture you weren't allowed to sit on and pictures of people wearing funny clothes. Turned out the last guy who lived in the house had a really weird name, Weeks Hall, and he was an artist. Since he went to all these art colleges, Mamma got real excited and wanted to study his paintings in the studio where they had them set up on easels. She'd never had the chance to go to art school, and she was biting her lips in this real anxious way, like it was the one thing in the world she wanted to do more than anything else. So I said I didn't mind.

I sneaked down the staircase and found the rear door to the backyard. The Bayou Teche meandered past the house. The air was clammy and moist. Sprinklers chugged in a circle, spattering the azaleas blossoming under the oak and camellia trees. Shadows-on-the-Teche had oak trees in the front and the back, dripping with moss, and I felt like I could breathe again, even if the afternoon was hotter than a firecracker.

Flinging off my shoes and socks, I ran down the stone steps to the paths winding around the shrubbery. I found a spot to sit by the water until I could go home.

I swear two hours went by, but I didn't have a watch.

"Livie, where have you been?" Mamma's sharp voice broke into my daydream. I'd been watching the slow progress of a turtle on a cypress knee near the bank.

He was almost to the top when Mamma yanked me to my feet.

"Where are your shoes, young lady?"

"I took them off."

"Where?"

"Um, up there somewhere." I pointed in the general direction, but Mamma's irritation rattled me so that I couldn't remember the exact spot.

"March back up there and find them. Now."

"I can go barefoot."

"Not with me you can't. Why do you have to be so defiant? Why do you have to be so ornery? You're so different from your sisters!"

Anger filled my throat. "I wouldn't be like Faye and Crickett if you paid me a million dollars!"

"I'm sure they feel the same way." Mamma stormed down the gravel path, shaking her head. Turning around, she squinted at me in the bright sunlight. "Don't matter what we do, we're always at each other's throats, aren't we, Olivia?" Her voice sounded quivery, as if she was trying not to cry.

I shrugged, wishing now that I'd never agreed to the day's outing. We'd been doomed from the get-go.

I scoured the huge mansion yard, but it didn't matter how long I looked, my shoes and socks had disappeared somewhere in the shrubbery of Shadows-on-the-Teche.

"Maybe the hedges ate them," I finally suggested.

"Very funny," Mamma said with another sigh. If I had a nickel for every one of her sighs, I'd be stinkin' rich.

We'd driven home in silence, the package containing the new yellow Easter dress crackling in its wrapper on the seat, like a wedge between us.

Secretly, I was pleased I didn't own dress shoes any longer, and I vowed I'd never wear Sunday shoes again. Not if I could help it.

A few days later, a brand-new pair of white, shiny dress shoes was sitting on my bedspread. Compliments of Mamma. I threw the shoe box into my closet.

Now I punched my pillow, remembering that the shopping trip happened only two weeks before Mamma's coma. We'd stayed mad at each other and never made up. I sniffed my pillow, smelling a whiff of Mamma's Prince Matchabelli perfume lingering in the slipcover. It made her feel close and yet farther away than ever.

I didn't think I'd gone to sleep, but sometime in the night I felt Daddy's big hands cupping my head like one of the priests giving someone a blessing in church.

I bolted upright. "Mamma!" The word blurted out, making me sound guilty. I didn't like knowing that my thoughts might spit right out of my mouth before I could stop them.

That old, regular life with Mamma was like a dream now—the coma had stolen it away—and I didn't know if it would ever come back, but every day I wished for a second chance. I'd tell her I loved her, but mostly I wanted her to say it back to *me*.

"Shh, shh," Daddy whispered.

I had no idea what time it was. Silvery moonlight draped the galerie like moss hanging from the oak trees. The porch was sweltering. Heat pulsed the air. The smell of sleep clung to my mouth. I felt my daddy's eyes on me, black as the coffee in his demitasse.

"I'm going froggin', Livie. You come with me?"

I sucked in my breath. When I jumped up, I hit my toes on the sandals lying on the floor, scattering them into the dresser. I heard my collection of glass frogs and gators on top of the dresser start to shiver from the collision, but they didn't fall over or break.

"Easy, Sugar Bee. Them frogs'll wait for us. They ain't going nowhere."

Quickly, I pulled on a long-sleeved cotton shirt and my overalls.

"Grab your boots," Daddy said.

Crickett rolled over in her sleep, flopping one arm across my side of the bed, the sheet bunched around her legs.

I slipped out the door, following Daddy's dark shape down to the dock, and clomped along in my rubber boots. They were a little big. Faye's castoffs. I think she'd worn them exactly once.

It was a perfect night for frogging. The air belched with loud deep-throated bullfrogs. If I wasn't careful I'd step on one. That wasn't really true, but that's how it felt.

Which meant we'd get a load of frogs tonight. Easy pickin's.

Daddy already had his own skiff outfitted and ready to go. He yanked the starter, and the motor purred like a panther. I unhooked the rope from the dock's piling and the boat drifted from the bank. Within moments, the back porch faded, disappearing into the night.

I always worried that the skiff's engine would cause the frogs to go hide. Or scare off the catfish or the turtles, making them hunker deeper down in the river, but it never did.

Daddy steered past the Landrys' dark, sleeping fishing shack, and then the Broussards' and the Heberts'. An image of T-Jacques Landry chopping firewood drifted through my mind, his shock of dark hair and the eyes that always stared deep into mine. I shook my head to erase the picture. I wasn't one of those girls who was going to go mooning over a boy. That'd be the day!

After another mile, there weren't any more houses or people. Just me and Daddy and the swamp. I studied his dark shadow in the aft of the boat and thought about how perfect the night was — if it weren't for Mamma's sleeping sickness. Nothing was right in my family, and I dreaded the day my sins were gonna catch up with me, but the bayou made me feel like the world was full of beauty and possibilities. Like someday, somehow, just *maybe*, I could be the girl I wanted to be.

"That little cove up ahead is where we'll go hunting," Daddy murmured. He steered the boat around a bend into a nook of towering moss-laden trees. Water hyacinth hugged the banks. A million stars ruled the blackness, glittering like Daddy's skinning knife. A swirling fog rose from the flat surface of the water.

"What time is it?"

"Past midnight, Sugar Bee."

"Aunt Colleen still with Mamma?"

"Don't you worry. Told Colleen it was bullfrog season and we needed the meat. Been listening to 'em for hours. Said she'd hold down the fort while we're gone." He pointed up ahead. "There — that's where they're hollering."

The closer the skiff got to the banks, the louder the bullfrogs belched. Grrrup! Grrrup! Grrruuuuup! Their throat sacs grew as they stretched with each cry. The bigger the throat sac, the deeper the sound, and there were some mighty big ones tonight. As if the world only contained frogs, millions of them.

I slapped at the air, then at my arms. A cloud of mosquitoes flew into my face. One even raced straight into my mouth. I spit into the water, and then ducked my head down, tightly shutting my lips. The closer we got to the banks, the thicker the mosquitoes got, too.

Daddy chuckled as he watched me flapping my arms. "Those 'squitoes so thick you gotta tie yourself to the boat so they don't carry you off."

"They aren't getting *me*," I retorted.

Daddy laughed again, then strapped the special flashlight around his forehead and flipped it on. A beam of white lit up the trees and shoreline. "Remember to look for the red eyes."

Almost immediately, I saw two red eyes sitting on the bank. "There's some frogs!"

"Nope, that's a gator. He's lying out in the water. Guess he wants supper, too."

Daddy revved the engine and the boat shot forward. "You gotta watch your sides. Them alligators can eat a boat if you're not looking."

Sweat trickled down the inside of my shirt, but I shivered at my daddy's words, thinking about my baby alligator. Would his mamma come looking for him? I didn't think so. Alligators had brains the size of a pea. He was lost for good. That's why he needed me to rescue him.

After another quarter of a mile, Daddy cut the engine. The skiff drifted slowly toward the thicket, bumping gently into branches and stumps, the air damp and slimy.

Daddy whispered, "See that up ahead, Livie? There's a whole clan of bullfrogs. Just waiting for us."

A row of red eyes lined up right along the bank. Grrrup! Grrruuuuup!

"Get out the gig, Sugar Bee."

I found the metal-pronged tool in the bottom of the boat. It was made for snagging a frog right where he sang. I stood up, crouching, ready to go.

"Remember, not too hard. Get him in the middle, not the legs."

The boat made a slurping sound as it slid closer to the bank's edge.

"Now, Livie!"

I reached out and speared a frog right in its middle, trying not to squeeze its guts too hard, but trying to hold on tight enough so it didn't slip out of the gig.

At the same moment, Daddy leaned over the boat and grabbed another bullfrog with his bare hands, right where it sat, its throat bulging like a balloon. With the other hand, he grabbed a second one. Then he struck the frog on the head to get it good and dazed so it wouldn't jump around the boat. Long, floppy legs dangled from his hands. Speckled frog skin shone under the lamplight.

"Three already," I said excitedly.

"Frogs' legs for supper tomorrow, Sugar Bee."

"Let's get some more!"

"Sounds like a plan, but right now we're heading out of here."

"But why? There are lots more frogs out there."

"Yep, but a cottonmouth's hanging close to your head and licking his chops to taste a pretty little girl. Think we'll scoot along and leave him be."

Quickly, Daddy pulled the cord of the motor and started the boat up again, reversing position. Branches and leaves crackled in the wake.

Behind me, I heard a tiny rustling and then a soft plop. The cottonmouth had slithered off the branch, looking for a warm, juicy hand to bite.

"Night might be the best time for frogging," Daddy added. "It's also the best time to get ate by a gator or bit by a snake."

"Look at them frogs there," I said when we pulled up along another inlet. I got the prong ready, but when I reached out to snag one, I stopped. The frog sat there on the bank, frozen stiff. His beady red eyes glowed under the lamplight. Even as I inched closer, that darn frog just sat there, throat sac bulging. He didn't even try to jump and escape his certain doom.

"It ain't moving," I said. "Is he dead?"

"Never seen no frog do that before," Daddy said, and he whistled softly between his teeth. "I do believe that bullfrog is paralyzed with fear."

I stared at it some more. The bullfrog gave me a funny feeling. I couldn't grab it with my metal prong, and I couldn't reach out with my hands, either. *Paralyzed.* What a strange word. Rolling that word around in my mouth gave me a funny feeling. That word fit Mamma. Her body was paralyzed in that hospital bed in the front room. So was her brain, which wouldn't do what it was supposed to anymore.

A prickly feeling ran up and down my spine. I think *paralyzed* described me, too. My mouth wouldn't open to tell the truth or spill my guilt.

"You wanna get him or leave him?" Daddy asked.

Softly, I said, "Leave him be."

"You okay, Livie girl?" Daddy asked as he retrieved the pole to push the boat along the shallow shoreline.

I nodded, not trusting myself to speak.

"You got awful quiet all of a sudden," Daddy added, but he didn't ask any more questions.

For another hour or so, he scouted the banks, following the bullfrogs' belching serenades. We finally had a pile of frogs in our sacks by the time we headed home.

I yawned as I lugged the bag of bullfrogs out of the boat.

"I'll take care of them, Sugar Bee," Daddy said. "You done great."

"I got eleven frogs," I said, dropping the bag on the grass. My toes were sweating inside the rubber boots. My arms had streaks of dried mud, and I felt a scratch on my cheek where a branch had licked me, but I didn't care.

"Yep, you're my little hunter. You go on to bed now. Morning will be here too soon."

"'Night, Daddy."

"'Night, Sugar Bee."

I wrapped my arms around Daddy's middle and he gave me a bear hug that squeezed all the yawns away. Squeezed the tears right out of my eyes, too, because I felt one roll down my cheek. It was safer to hug him in the dark where he couldn't see my eyes or my face.

Ducking my head, I walked up the edge of the bank, my chest aching. I didn't want the night to end. I tried not to think about how my daddy's love might slip away, like water between my fingers, when he found out the truth about me.

Out of the blackness, something ran smack into me. I shrieked. "Who's that?"

"Me, Thibodaux."

"What are you doing up in the middle of the night?" I demanded.

He ignored the question and asked his own. "Where you been?"

I blew against my bangs. "Frogging with Daddy."

"Hey, T-Boy," Daddy said, unloading the boat. "Can't sleep?"

"No, sir."

"Want to go frogging sometime with us?"

"Oh, yes, sir," Thibodaux said eagerly.

"We'll get you out of bed next time," Daddy said. He walked up the grass with his tackle box and gear.

When Daddy was out of earshot, Thibodaux said in a low voice, "You're a daddy's boy, aren't you?"

"I ain't no boy, you stupid!"

"Did I say that?" He acted all innocent.

I tried not to let him get to me. "I could put a shot between your eyes, Thibodaux Benoit," I told him with quiet satisfaction.

"Very funny. You don't even own a good gun. Just toy guns."

"You don't know much, T-Boy, do you?" I said. "Got me a twenty-two for hunting and a BB gun for bugs." I couldn't stop myself from bragging. This kid made me so angry I just wanted to prove he was wrong.

He smiled like he had a secret, and I wanted to wipe the smirk off his face with my fist. Then my heart pounded as I realized what he'd just said. "Hey, when were you trespassing in my room looking at my guns? Did you touch them? You better not!"

T-Boy looked guilty as heck, but he denied it. "Why would I go into a girl's perfume-stinkin', fluffy bedroom?"

"My bedroom doesn't have perfume or fluff!" I said through clenched teeth. Except for Crickett's side with her dolls and frilly vanity table and the dollhouse, but I didn't tell him that. "You are a liar, Thibodaux Benoit."

My cousin didn't seem to care what I called him. He pressed on. "Owning those guns just proves you're more boy than girl."

I felt my eyes sting as his words struck a nerve. Sometimes I wished I was a boy. Life would be a whole lot easier. Mamma could stop bugging me about becoming a young lady, and I wouldn't have to worry about being an ugly girl for the rest of my life. A girl who would rather mend a trap or shoot a squirrel, clean a shotgun or dig for worms any day. I was trapped like a crab in a cage between the world of boys and the world of girls. I didn't belong in either side completely.

"You're going to end up sixteen years old and only know how to shoot nutria, Olivia," Mamma'd yell out the back door. "That might be fine when you're eight or nine, but not when you're a young lady."

"Only matters if I *want* to be a young lady," I yelled back. Sometimes I got my mouth washed out with soap for talking back. One time I was grounded during Daddy's winter hunting trip.

I could feel anger rising higher and higher in my chest. I'd come home, feeling close to Daddy for the first time in a week, and now my annoying cousin was spoiling my whole frogging night.

"Livie's a boy, Livie's a boy," Thibodaux jeered, wearing an evil grin. He knew he'd hit a sore spot and he was playing it for all it was worth.

"Just shut up," I hissed back, waving my fists in the air. His words conjured up the day of Mamma's accident all over again. She and I had gotten into an argument on our way to take a meal to Mrs. Hebert, a sick neighbor. It was another one of her attempts at making me more of a girl. I cringed when I thought about how I'd stood up in my pirogue, swinging my paddle over my head and shouting, "I hate my life! I hate being a girl! I hate you!"

T-Boy kicked at the grass, then threw a rock across the black water as hard as he could. "This stupid bayou is dirty and it stinks," he shot off.

I let out my breath in a gasp and took a step forward. Now he was insulting the world I loved best, the bayou that was beautiful and safe. A place where I could run and it loved me back no matter what. Daddy often said, "You love the swamp so much, Livie, I think you been drinkin' too much of that bayou water."

Thibodaux reached down and pulled up an elephant ear, scattering the pieces of the leaves in the water. "I hate it here!" he added with venom.

I swung around and, before I knew it, I'd shoved Thibodaux with both hands. It felt so good to give him a good push, but my cousin was caught off guard. He was also lighter than I expected, because next thing I knew he'd gone sprawling straight into the river.

He came up spluttering and cussing up a storm. "I'm going to get you!" He flapped his arms and crawled up the bank. Before I could take a step backward, Thibodaux had reached out and grabbed my ankle, making me lose my balance. He was surprisingly strong and dragged me down the edge of the bank and into the river. My head went under, and I got a mouth full of bayou mud.

As I was flailing my hands trying to break the surface, a strong pair of arms grabbed me under the shoulders and hauled me out of the water. I lay on the bank coughing, my hair plastered all over my face, which meant I couldn't see at all.

"I'm gonna get you for this!" I yelled.

"Who you gonna get, Livie?" Daddy asked, towering above me.

"That—Thibodaux," I choked.

"I think you done dunked him good. You kids are a couple of soaked cats tearing into each other."

I could hear T-Boy breathing hard next to me in the darkness.

"Maybe now you're both cooled off," Daddy said in a voice laced with disappointment. My skin crawled with shame for fighting and throwing Thibodaux into the bayou right in front of my father's eyes.

"I don't know what you're fighting about, but you both better be in bed asleep in five minutes or you'll have to spend the whole day together tomorrow, I garon-tee. Me, I think that'd be a good punishment."

"Yes, Daddy," I said, running up the grass. I was furious at Thibodaux, and I was pretty sure I was begin-ning to hate him. Spending an entire day with him was the last thing I wanted to do. Daddy sure knew how to make punishment hurt.

In the bedroom, I took off the muddy boots and soggy clothes, leaving them by the back door, then wiped myself dry with a towel, put on my pajamas, and crawled into bed next to Crickett. Her legs and arms were splayed all over the mattress. I pushed her to the other side, then fell back onto my pillow.

Tears slipped out, rolling down my hot cheeks. My pillow was getting waterlogged from my wet hair and now my eyes would finish the job. Thibodaux had ruined everything, all the good things that had happened that night. It was almost like he'd stolen my daddy from me, the person I was afraid of losing more than anybody else.

When I finally fell asleep, I dreamed I was ate by an alligator. Every last piece of me got swallowed up. Gulp. Gone. It seemed fitting.

Chapter 8

"BREAKFAST IN FIFTEEN MINUTES!" AUNT COLLEEN called out the next morning.

"No breakfast for me!" I said as I whipped the front door closed and jumped down from the porch. I didn't care about breakfast. After last night's fight, I couldn't face my father, either. He might not even speak to me, and that would be worse than him yelling at me or looking at me with disappointment.

I'd also woken up with a plan. If I hurried, I could make it back before I was missed too much.

Green stalks of sugarcane were growing in the moist sun. Dust kicked up in small puffs along the road, and my sandals made a funny burping sound with each step. I scratched at a bug bite on my leg and then two more on my ankle.

After I passed the town limit sign for Bayou Bridge, the shops came into view: Verret's Café, Marie's Market, Pete's Gas-Up, and Ozaire's Laundromat. There was also the post office, Pierre's Hardware, and Sweet Ellen's Bakery, but that was pretty much the whole town. Small houses were scattered up and down the side streets and the school was down by the park, but I didn't even glance in that direction.

At St. Paul's, I stopped at the double doors to catch my breath. Sweat ran down the back of my neck and I lifted my hair to cool my skin. "Oh, shoot. I forgot to comb my hair," I said to myself. "And that green ribbon would have made me look halfway presentable."

"I think you look good just like you are," a boy's voice said behind me.

I spun around on my heels so fast I almost choked. T-Jacques Landry was standing right behind me, a broom in his hand, and a ball cap pulled down over his black eyes, which gleamed at me from under the brim.

My cheeks starting burning. He'd caught me talking to myself! And looking a mess. I couldn't even remember if I'd washed my face. Probably not, if I forgot about brushing my hair.

I squared my shoulders and tried to compose myself. What did I care how I looked? It was only that T-Jacques Landry.

"How you do, Livie?" he asked, and his voice was deeper than I remembered from last school year. Which made me feel lopsided, like I wouldn't be able to walk straight if I took another step toward the church door. Which T-Jacques was now blocking.

"What are *you* doing here?" I spat back as soon as I could think.

He held up his broom as if I couldn't already see it. "I help Father John with sweeping and planting flowers and stuff. Just going for the lawn mower when I saw you."

"Oh." I paused. "You mean to cut the grass." I must have gotten sunstroke because words were coming out of my mouth like my brain had turned into a bowl of mush.

He grinned, and I almost wanted to sock him.

"You laughing at me, T-Jacques Landry?"

He wiped the smile off his face and looked at me with the most serious expression I'd ever seen on a boy. "I'd never laugh at you, Livie Mouton."

The shade of the doorway suddenly felt hotter than an oven. "Father John here?" I finally asked.

"Yep, he's inside. Go on in if you want. You don't have to knock."

"I know *that*."

I stepped forward, and he finally moved half a foot to the right to let me pass. "I hope I get to see you sometime in that green hair ribbon, Livie."

"Well, that'd be your lucky day, T-Jacques Landry."

He gave me another one of his slow grins. "Yep."

Just that one word got me flustered. A hot flush crept up my neck as I inched toward the church doors, battling hard as I could to stay cool and collected. "So why're you working for the priest anyway?"

He pushed back his cap. "Broke Father John's office window in the back there. Behind the gardens."

"Doing what?"

"Pitching a softball. What else?"

"Maybe you better practice your aim," I told him as I grasped the heavy door handle and pulled.

T-Jacques's fingers brushed mine when he reached out to help me open the door.

"I can do it myself!"

"See you on the bayou sometime?" he asked. "In your pirogue?"

My heart jumped a beat as I ducked my head, not knowing what to say to his question, so I pulled the door shut before he could ask me anything else.

The entrance was dark; I had to wait a minute to let my eyes adjust. It was cool and airy and beautiful inside the church. I'd always loved the stained glass pictures, so I paused to admire them while I tried to slow down my pulse. My heart was pounding and my head was reeling like I'd just sprinted a mile. All because of T-Jacques. Which made no sense at all, but I didn't want to think about what it might mean or why I felt like this every time I saw him.

Stepping farther inside the vestibule, I tried to settle the butterflies in my stomach and get my bearings. It was hard to put T-Jacques out of my mind so I could concentrate on why I was here, since I kept picturing his grin with the hint of a dimple on the left corner of his mouth. He just made you want to smile back, and I had to focus really hard on not lifting my lips and showing any teeth when I was around him. In case he got the wrong idea.

I blew out my breath and focused my thoughts toward helping Mamma wake up. Should I go to the confessional box in the corner? The curtains were closed, meaning that Father John was inside with someone. A moment later a young man pulled back the drape of the booth, walked down the aisle, and lit a candle before exiting the church.

That was a good idea. Digging a quarter from my pocket, I bought one of the candles, too, sticking the coin in the box. I picked the tallest candle sitting on the table. Tall for Mamma. Tall for long lasting. I lit the wick and watched the orange flame sizzle, feeling the warmth in the musty-smelling church. Then I set the candle next to the others on the table and kneeled to make the sign of the cross.

I tried to remember one of the prayers Mamma always said, but for some reason it just didn't seem strong enough for the tangled mess I was in.

"Please, God," I began, wondering if I could say my own personal prayer. I tried to make my voice as soft as possible so no one else could hear, even though the church was empty. "Please make Mamma better. Please help her wake up. Help her know I didn't mean to hurt her, not really, I was just so—"

"Livie—" A man's voice spoke next to me.

I knocked into the table and hot wax spilled, making little puddles on the tablecloth. "Oh, I'm sorry!" I cried, and my voice seemed to echo up to the rafters. I wanted to melt into the floor like the candle wax.

Father John gazed down at me with his bald, shiny head. Only a small tuft of hair was left on top, and his face was crisscrossed with a weaving of tiny wrinkles. But it was a good face. Serene and peaceful. Like he hadn't just read the Bible, but he'd eaten the pages with all those stories of Jesus and it was living inside him. "No harm done, Livie. I'm sorry I startled you."

"I was just—" I stopped, staring at his elegant black robes. The church felt too magnificent for my shorts and silly, burping sandals.

"Lighting a candle for your mother?" he asked.

I nodded.

"Did you say a prayer, too?"

"Yes," I whispered, even though I hadn't had a chance to finish.

"God wants us to come to Him when we need His help. He'll help your family get through this crisis. I pray He'll give you the strength your family needs."

"Thank you," I said. "I better go now."

"I hear your aunt is here to help. She's a nurse?"

I nodded again.

"It must be a comfort to have her help. God sends us blessings even during our trials, doesn't He?"

I had never thought about Aunt Colleen being a blessing. She seemed more nosy with a penchant for mind probing. I pictured Aunt Colleen peeling back the skin of my brain to reveal all my secret thoughts and acts. I shivered, but maybe that was the church's air-conditioning.

"I'll have to think about that," I finally admitted. Then I realized that my words didn't sound very charitable. Maybe I needed to do more praying and Bible eating myself.

Father John let out a laugh. "Out of the mouths of babes!"

I had no idea what he was talking about. "I'm not a baby."

"That's true, Miss Livie Mouton. I just meant that I liked your honesty. Always be honest. With yourself, with your family, and with God."

I looked up at him, wondering what he knew. Could God tell Father John about me? Was that possible? I hadn't told any outright lies, I was only keeping a secret, but it was the worst secret in the world.

"Journey home safely then," Father John said. "Tell your father hello."

I glanced at the altar to make sure the candle I'd lit

was still glowing. I could smell the smokiness in the air and felt a fleeting moment of comfort. I'd finally done something to help Mamma, even if it was just one small flame on a single white candle.

"I'll make sure it stays lit for you," he said, following my glance. "Most important, if you have something weighing on your mind, confession can be a good place to get rid of your burden."

I swallowed. Was the word *guilty* written all over my face? Maybe I needed to look in a mirror. Going to confession sounded spooky. I just couldn't see myself sitting in a cupboard talking to a wall. I'd never done it before, and I didn't think I wanted to start.

Father John gave me a knowing look. "God can forgive through the blood of His son, Jesus Christ."

I nodded, but his words just gave me more to worry about. As I backed out of the heavy doors, heat closed around me like a blanket from a hot dryer. The sun blinded my eyes after the dusky church. I glanced around. The lawns and gardens were tranquil and quiet. Roses bloomed along the stone wall. A sprinkler chugged in one corner. I found myself thinking how it was T-Jacques who took care of those roses. That sprinkler. Those ornery weeds starting to poke up through the sidewalks. I had to admit, he done a good job. I wanted to lie on the cool grass under the sprawling oak leaves and take a nap. After T-Jacques left for the day, that is.

Listening to the spinning sprinklers made it all seem normal and fine. Just like it was supposed to.

But everything was not fine, and I wasn't sure if anything in my life would ever be normal again. I'd broken that commandment about being nice to your parents and doing what they told you. If Mamma died, I would have killed her. I'd be a murderer. Another broken commandment. The worst one of all. The one that sent you down there forever.

Penance for a broken window was a thousand times easier than this. I didn't see how there could be any atonement for hurting your own mother so bad she never woke up again . . . or she died.

A sob stuck in my throat. The secret seemed to own

me, dragging on my mind. Even if I spilled my guts, it wouldn't bring Mamma back. It wouldn't change Mamma floating upside down in the bayou, her hair drifting along the current like hyacinth petals.

Maybe it *was* too late to try to help or fix it. There were some things that couldn't be undone, no matter how sorry we were later.

My nose was running and I kept wiping it with the back of my hand as I traced my path back through town. I'd taken the first step though, even if it was a small one, and I felt anxious to start the next part of my plan, even if it was dangerous and I didn't come back alive. Which would serve me right, I guess. My life for my mamma's life. So I could give her back to Daddy and my sisters, the people she loved best.

"Livie!" Jeannie came out of the grocery store and we almost bumped into each other. "What are you doing?" She stuck a plastic bag into the basket of her bike and I could see white bread, bananas, and Frosted Flakes peeking out from the top.

I blinked my eyes clear and pretended I was happy. "Went to church to light a candle for Mamma."

"That's a good idea." Jeannie leaned against her bike and gave a huge, bored yawn. "It's already been a week of summer vacation and we haven't even done anything fun yet. Let's think up something."

"I got something really big to do right now, Jeannie."

"Sounds exciting. What is it?"

"I'm going to the *traiteur*'s house out in the swamp."

Jeannie almost dropped her bicycle. "Are you crazy?"

I started talking faster. "Maybe she's got a cure. Some sort of sleeping-sickness herb." I felt like a drowning person grasping at weeds and loose branches, even as they floated out of reach.

Jeannie frowned. "I don't know about any herb for a coma. More like warts and headaches. Besides, she might turn us into cockroaches."

I smiled at her joke and crossed my fingers behind my back. If Jeannie came with me, going into the swamp wouldn't be quite so frightening.

I watched her take a gulp as she added, "Our parents will kill us if they find out."

"I know," I said. I couldn't ask her to come with me on such a dangerous mission, although I wanted her to something fierce.

Our eyes met and Jeannie reached out to grasp my hand. "I wouldn't do this for nobody else," she told me.

My heart twisted with love for her. "Now I know why you're my best friend, Jeannie Martin."

Half an hour later, my legs were shaking as I untied the ropes from the dock. "Hurry," I said in a low voice so we wouldn't attract Crickett or T-Boy's attention. Sitting down, I steadied the pirogue, my heart pounding like the drum in Paw Paw's band.

I hoped I didn't drop dead of fright once we arrived at Miz Allemond's house. I'd remembered her name when I woke up that morning, and it was like a sign that I was supposed to go. Was she a true *traiteur*, a healer — or did she do hoodoo magic like the kids at school said? I had to take the chance. After all, Mamma had gone to see her, and she didn't come back as a dung beetle or sporting a third eyeball.

At the cypress cove, I stopped to scoop up T-Baby from under the elephant ears and rubbed my finger along the ridges of his back. "We have a quest," I told him. I figured I could use him to clamp his teeth into the *traiteur*'s arm if she tried to give us antennae or horns.

"I'll bet you're the only girl in Louisiana with a pet alligator," Jeannie said, reaching out to touch his tiny webbed foot.

Taming a gator *was* a bit like a miracle. Now I just wanted one of those miracles for Mamma. "Ready?" I asked.

Jeannie's fingers curled around the edge of the pirogue, her knuckles turning white. I felt bad about dragging her along with me, but I tried to focus on helping Mamma get better to make up for my horrible past.

Pushing the guilt down my gut, I stuck the pole in the water and dug in, setting off for the deepest, darkest part of the swamp.

Chapter 9

I POLED UNTIL MY ARMS ACHED.

Mirage Allemond lived on the edge of the Bayou Teche, at the spot where the bayou narrowed into swampland. Daddy had always told me never to go beyond this point, but he'd never actually forbidden me to go to Miz Allemond's house itself.

I maneuvered the pirogue through the tight channel past an outhouse, a mess of chicken coops, and a muskrat dam springing up out of the river with mounds of twigs and leafy branches.

"Ever wonder what it's like to live in a muskrat dam?" Jeannie said.

"Cozy and warm, I'll bet. Secret tunnels and tiny rooms. And only you knowing the entrance and exit." I pretended this was only a casual river stroll—that we weren't on our way to the most perilous house in the swamp.

I poled around a bend in the river and we drifted

through a graveyard of ancient cypress stumps. Hundreds of them like corpses.

"This place is creepy," Jeannie whispered as we slid under a curtain of thick moss.

I agreed with her, but my throat was so dry, I couldn't get out a single word. The channel narrowed again, the trees getting even denser. Cypress and tupelo grew so thick, sunlight didn't even pierce the branches.

"Don't you think we better go back?" Jeannie said a moment later. "My mamma's always telling me not to take risks. Ride my bike safely—"

"Look both ways before crossing a street," I added. "And Miss Beaumont was always saying—"

Jeannie and I both spoke at the same time: "Never run with scissors!"

"Two years ago my mamma went all by herself to get a healing for Crickett. Now I gotta go into danger for her."

"I guess it's different when you do it for someone you love," Jeannie said in a small voice, as if she knew she wasn't going to talk me out of it. "Like someone jumping in front of a bus to save their child."

I turned around to look at her. She had a dirt mark on her cheek and her skin looked pale and sweaty.

"Thanks for jumping in front of the bus for me," I told her.

She tried to smile. "You're welcome. But you're the one gonna get run over. I ain't going in that *traiteur*'s house with you."

Taking a risk for someone you love, no matter how dangerous it was. I liked the sound of that, and I held on to that thought as I poled the pirogue through clutches of dark green waterweeds.

A massive oak branch swept across the water like a gigantic arm, as if reaching for us. "Duck!" I cried as we barely missed scraping our heads.

The mud was so deep it was hard to pole through. My hands were bright red and getting blisters. I wanted to turn around and go back home. Would I be too tired to get us back? We could end up stuck in the middle of the swamp miles from home. I promised myself that if we didn't find the *traiteur*'s house in five more minutes I was turning around, but when I looked up again there it was, the *traiteur*'s house sitting smack-dab in the middle of the swamp on a tiny island with trees and shrubs so thick I'd have sworn we'd landed in the jungle.

A rusted corrugated tin roof sat like a hat on four leaning walls. The rickety porch had caved in — a yawning, sinister mouth.

Crawfish nets littered the yard. A half-sunken dock swayed in the murky water. Two boats, one partially submerged, were tied there. Broken crates, old paddles, poles, pieces of scrap lumber, scrambled fishing lines, and wooden water barrels lay all over the place.

I laid my pole across my knees and shivered in the gloom. The place was dead quiet. Nothing moved. The air was slow and muggy, not even a breeze to stir the leaves.

"Livie!" Jeannie moaned.

I knew what she was thinking. We were crazy to come here, but I also felt a surge of accomplishment. We'd made it through the swamp without sinking the pirogue or being swallowed by a twelve-footer. Maybe there were some things I could do pretty good.

I stroked my alligator across the head. "Hey, T-Baby," I said and my voice sounded loud in the heavy stillness. The baby gator looked at me with half-closed eyes. It was high noon and naptime. I fed him a bite of shrimp from my pocket to keep him happy and brushed him with cool water.

The pirogue seemed to get a mind of its own, almost like an invisible hand guiding it through the cypress knees until it bumped the dock. I slowly wrapped the rope around one of the bobbing piles and tied a knot.

Jeannie whispered, "I don't like this place."

Me neither, but I didn't tell her that. "Knocking on that door can't be any worse than the haunted house the high school kids put on at Halloween. Remember when the ghouls grabbed your legs and those vampires showed us bloody eyeballs in a dish?"

"I remember," Jeannie said slowly.

We didn't remind each other about how much we'd screamed. Now I tried to swallow, but my throat was dry as dust. My heart pounded like it was going to jump right out of my chest.

Maybe this was part of my penance. Trudging through the swamp roads might be the only way to help Mamma — maybe it was the road to forgiveness, too.

When I got to my feet, I swore there were eyes watching me. The shack looked deserted, but a boat tied to the pilings usually meant a person was home, even if the boat was half sunk.

Cradling T-Baby in the crook of my arm, I stepped out and then held the boat for Jeannie. The alligator nipped my finger, then closed his eyes and fell asleep. What an easy life.

I shivered, my knees knocking together. I could feel them eyes again. Someone was watching us.

The front door creaked open a sliver and a pair of black eyes fixed on me as I walked forward. I opened my mouth to call out a little hello, but my voice had disappeared. The urge to run was so strong I could taste it, like sour milk. I took a step backward, squeezing T-Baby for a tiny bit of comfort, and accidentally stepped on Jeannie's foot.

"Oh, yee-yi!" she cried out.

"Ssh!" I hissed back. I wanted to hold hands like we used to in kindergarten when Jeannie and I skipped rope. *Cinderella dressed in yellow, Went upstairs to kiss a fellow, Made a mistake and kissed a snake, How many doctors did it take?* Kindergarten was easy days compared to now.

I took a breath and croaked out, "Miz Allemond? I came to ask for your help, ma'am."

A shadow moved behind the door. "Who're you?"

"I'm Livie—I mean, Olivia Mouton. My daddy is Jean Baptiste Mouton. We live north up the Bayou Teche, ma'am, near Bayou Bridge."

"What you got there in your hands?"

"This here is T-Baby. He's my alligator."

There was a harrumph and then the voice came again. "So's you some kind of brave little girl?"

My heart jammed up my throat. "No, ma'am."

"Now that's a fib if I ever heard one. Don't it take a brave girl to have an alligator for a pet and pole that pirogue all the way out to see Miz Mirage Allemond?" The voice in the shadows chuckled. "I'd say that's pretty brave. Or plumb crazy."

My eyes watered and I sniffed, wiping my hand across my nose. Right now, I wanted to be home, safe in one of Daddy's bear hugs. I wanted Mamma to wake up more than anything else I'd ever wanted. Ever. I wanted my old life back—not this horrible, never-ending awfulness of knowing Mamma might never be the same again. I wanted to be a different person, one who would never hurt anybody again. I guess there was one thing I'd learned today. I couldn't go backward, no matter how much I wanted to. I could only go forward.

"Well, dontcha think you better come on up here if you want my help?"

I put my foot onto the first step of the porch, even though I was shaking like a ninny.

"Hold on," the woman said. "You ain't bringin' that reptile in here. No matter how cute he is."

"What should I do?"

"See that bucket? Put him in there and leave him by the front door. He'll be fine. And there's a bit of water to keep him cool."

I carried T-Baby over to the bucket at the end of the porch and let him slip out of my arms. He fit just right, but he looked up at me with his sad alligator eyes. "Don't be a baby, T-Baby. I won't be long. You be good now, y'hear?"

Jeannie had stopped long before the porch, and I knew she wasn't going to take a single step closer. She was chewing so hard on her lips they were bright red.

Miz Allemond opened the screen door wider. "I ain't going to bite, but your friend needs to stay outside while we conduct business, Miss Olivia. I'll need your full attention."

Me and Jeannie stared at each other. Jeannie looked relieved. And then she looked guilty.

"It's okay," I told her. "Keep T-Baby company."

Jeannie whispered to me, "If I hear screaming I'll come in and save you."

I smiled weakly. "Okay."

"Miss Martin," Miz Allemond added, "you can sit under the tree while you wait, or if it rains you can take cover here on the porch."

I finished climbing the rickety porch steps, wondering if I'd ever see Jeannie again, and slowly walked past the threshold. Then my mouth dropped open. The parlor was completely draped in silvery-gray Spanish moss. There was moss everywhere: all over the furniture, the chairs, hanging off lamps and even the picture frames on the walls. Like the swamp had invaded the house.

"I pick it off the trees and dry it," Miz Allemond explained. "Gotta leave it inside until the threat of rain is gone. Least I got the bugs and spiders out of it first."

"What rain?" I asked. The day had been completely clear and now it was late afternoon. Even though there were a few clouds in the sky, if it was going to rain, it would have started by now.

Not ten seconds later, a clap of thunder cracked over-head, jarring the little house like it had been punched. Raindrops chattered across the corrugated tin roof.

Miz Allemond glanced up at the ceiling. "That rain."

She led me to the kitchen table where she was string-ing brooms from the dried moss. Miz Allemond was much younger than I thought, not much older than Mamma. Her skin was olive-colored, and her black hair had grown so long it was clear past the waistband of her purple dress.

Tiny little braids decorated her twisty, unruly hair just like a basket weaving. Strings of beads hung around her neck, and bracelets clacked around her wrists. Flying herons fashioned from silver dangled from her earlobes.

Mirage Allemond didn't wear a speck of makeup, but her lips were dark red and her eyelashes long and curly. As her hands worked the moss, her nostrils flared every time she breathed in and out.

She cocked her chin at me. "Not what you were expecting?"

I shook my head as she tied off a piece of twine with

her teeth, tossing her long hair over one shoulder. "If I'd known you were coming I'd-a worn my black witch costume." She chuckled, then winked at me and went to the stove to pour two cups of hot tea. The liquid was a strange dark green color. "Sugar?" she asked.

I stared at the cup. "No, thank you," I said in my best manners.

The *traiteur* laughed. "I'm not going to poison a little girl. Besides, if you notice, both cups are out of the same pot." She took a sip and closed her eyes. "I call it swamp tea. It's made up of nice, good herbs and will make you feel better."

Cautiously, I took a tiny sip. The tea tasted like mossy green grass.

I jumped as a brown-feathered sparrow suddenly swooped in from the front room and perched on Miz Allemond's shoulder.

"This is Winifred. Winnie for short. Isn't she a love?" Miz Allemond turned her face to the bird and let it kiss her on the cheek. "Now leave us be, Winnie, while we talk business."

The sparrow cocked its head, and then flew off again to settle on a pillow, mashing its spindly feet into the softness like it was a cat kneading with its paws.

"Look up there and you'll see Mister Lenny," Miz Allemond said, pointing. "He's my barn owl up in the corner on the bookshelf."

I leaned forward. Sure enough, blending in with the dark wood of the bookcase, an owl perched on a stick, still as a glass figurine. I wasn't sure he was an actual bird and wondered if Miz Allemond was pulling my leg. Then the owl's eyes blinked long and slow. Mister Lenny was *real*.

"I don't have pets like most folks. Dogs are too noisy and a cat would eat Winnie, but sick muskrats, squirrels, and coons, even nutria find their way to me. I patch 'em up and do a cure. They just want to be loved, you know."

I shook my head. I didn't know.

"Most people don't have a clue that nutrias are very friendly and make a good pet. They just kill and skin 'em. Ten dollars a pelt." Miz Allemond sipped her tea again.

My mind was racing as she talked. How did a person ask for a healing? Was I already supposed to know what I wanted, like when you asked for strings of licorice or a soda at the drugstore? Prices were posted in a store, but this was just a regular kitchen — if you didn't count the Spanish moss and the owl and sparrow.

Miz Allemond leaned back in her chair. "You've probably heard about my mamma who's been a healer in this swamp since she was a young married girl. My mamma's the one folks talk about. Wild gray hair that looked like a rat combed it; wrinkles so deep you could lose your finger in 'em. Black dress, floppy boots. She looked like a royal voodoo queen, like old Marie Laveau from way back when. Even though voodoo priestesses and *traiteurs* have absolutely nothing in common."

I studied my tea, letting it grow cold. I was embarrassed to answer. I couldn't tell Miz Allemond that her mamma was exactly who the kids at school were afraid of. Not somebody pretty like she was, in her purple gypsy dress and silver earrings.

"Well, Olivia, I have to make a confession," Miz Allemond went on solemnly. "My mamma's been passed on close to six months now. Most folks don't know that. People's tongues like to wag, and I let 'em. I couldn't care less what people say."

My heart sank as deep as the bayou mud. "You mean she's dead?"

"The priest buried her in the church graveyard, but before she left this world, my mamma cured hundreds of folks. She had a magical gift—a divine gift for healing. It comes from God, you know. One of those gifts the Bible talks about. We all have one. Gifts, I mean. Although some people get lucky because they get more than one."

I'd come all this way for nothing? The real *traiteur*, the real Miz Allemond, was dead and gone and buried? I pushed my hands against my eyes, but the tears were leaking anyway. Leaking away like the last bit of hope I'd been hanging on to.

Miz Allemond watched me. "My mamma was special. One of the best *traiteurs* in the swamp. She knew all the herbs and prayers. Trained by her grandfather way back when. Oh, my, she was something else."

"Yes, ma'am," I said, and scooted back my chair. "Guess I better be on my way home. I'm sorry to bother you."

Mirage Allemond blinked. "What are you talking about, child?"

"I—I needed help, but with your mamma passed on I've just taken up your time. I'm very sorry, truly I am."

When I started to get up, Miz Allemond pressed her hands down over mine, pinning my fingers to the table. A jolt raced up my arms.

"I don't think you understand, Miss Olivia." Her voice changed. It was powerful and commanding now. No more tea chitchat or old-time memories.

"What you don't understand is that I also possess the gift for healing. What's more—I have the power even stronger than my mamma did. When she passed me the gift, she lost it herself. That's the way of it. When the gift is given to the next generation, the first person doesn't own it any longer."

She released my hands and folded her palms together, staring at me across the table. I became conscious all over again of my dirty shirt and my tangled, ribbon-less hair.

"Your mamma's bad sick, ain't she?"

All the air left my lungs. "How did you know that? Did your power tell you?"

Miz Allemond laughed and her rich voice sounded delicious. She took my hand again and stroked my fingers one by one. Her skin was soft, even though her hands looked worn and stained, the nails broken. "I don't practice black magic, if that's what you mean. Don't own any crystal ball, either. Word about something like your mamma gets around. Even back here in the swamp where hardly a soul ever roams — except little girls looking for a cure."

I felt the tears start up again, and I couldn't help wondering what Miz Allemond would think of me if she knew the truth about Mamma's accident and the truth about me.

"It's okay, honey," Miz Allemond said soothingly. "Sometimes you just gotta let some tears out or you'll burst."

She handed me a tissue, and I wiped my eyes, and then blew my nose. "Will you come with me to heal my mamma?"

Miz Allemond shook her head. "Oh, no, I couldn't do that. I don't leave here much. My animals need me. I only shop a couple times a year, and the mail boat brings my groceries along with the bills."

"But if you don't come, how can you heal her?"

Miz Allemond gave a delicate laugh. "Oh, sweetie, *I'm* not going to heal her. I'm going to help *you* heal your mamma."

Her words knocked the air right out of me for the second time in two minutes.

Miz Allemond rose from her chair, poured my cup of cold green tea back into the pot, and left the room with a wink.

I listened to the clock ticking on the stove. Chicken and sausage gumbo in an okra roux simmered over a low gas flame and the smell made my stomach growl. I remembered that I hadn't eaten breakfast, and I wondered how Jeannie and T-Baby were doing out in the rain under the porch. We'd probably missed lunch, too.

Miz Allemond returned carrying a small oblong box. Ornate carvings of Oriental flowers and mystical dragons decorated the dark wood. Small jewels were glued along the sides, glittering in the shadowy kitchen.

The *traiteur* rested her hands on the lid of the box, but she didn't open it. "I'm going to give you a charm for your mother, but first there's a spell you need to do before you get home. Follow my instructions exactly: Get several big handfuls of moss and make yourself a necklace. While you wear the moss necklace, row your little pirogue in a circle ten times—backward. Try not to get dizzy." She smiled at me, but I was concentrating so hard my own smile felt funny on my face.

"You're a serious one, aren't you?" Miz Allemond

said, and I wondered if she was laughing at me. "I guess I'd be a solemn-faced child if my mamma had the sleeping sickness."

I jerked my chin up. Miz Allemond had just called Mamma's coma the sleeping sickness. How strange was that? The longer I was here, the more I liked her. I wanted to explore her house, pet the animals, eat her gumbo, and sleep on a moss-filled mattress.

"Be sure and row your boat in front of your own house," Miz Allemond added. "Without the alligator. And without Miss Jeannie Martin. Just yourself— alone. Then tie up the boat with your left hand, wrapping the rope to the left."

"Yes, ma'am," I said, memorizing her instructions and staring at the jeweled treasure box. I was dying to know what was inside.

"Now then, let's see what we have here." Miz Allemond lifted the lid and I tried to peek, but she kept the contents shielded. A moment later, a piece of yellow string about eight inches long appeared with knots tied into it. I counted eight knots and then she moved her fingers like a magician and a ninth knot appeared at the end.

"This string has been dipped in healing herbs like rosemary and ancient myrrh, Olivia. It's also been blessed with holy water from Father John. Bet that comes as a surprise to you." Miz Allemond chuckled again. "You're going to tie the string around your mamma's ankle. As you tie the string, say nine prayers. One prayer for each knot."

"I thought knotted-string cures were only used on babies," I said. "Mamma's a grown-up."

"But your mamma's sleeping just like a baby," Miz Allemond explained. "She don't know anything going on around her, ain't that right?"

That was true. I thought of something else. "Daddy mashed up her food and tried to feed her with a spoon. But he had to stop because she started choking—people in comas can't eat regular. We had to get more bags of that IV food."

"There you go, then. She's just like a child again. A sleeping child who cannot wake up, who probably can't even dream because her mind has become paralyzed."

My eyes darted to the *traiteur*'s face. Paralyzed, like the frogs the night before.

"We could try more complicated cures, but I think this one will work. I truly do believe this is the one. And it's the simplest, too."

I suddenly sat up. "Oh, no, I forgot to bring you any money for your services."

Miz Allemond waved her hands and her face looked stricken. "No, no, no, don't talk about payment, don't ever mention that, not during the giving of the cure. It might affect the potency of what I'm giving you."

I instantly clamped my mouth shut. I needed all the potency I could get.

"Now this spell needs two more ingredients. Well, several more, actually."

I wondered if Miz Allemond was going to brew roadkill guts or cut off a rat's tail.

"I'm sending you on a quest. You need to find nine items of your mamma's. Things that are special to her — and her alone. So it can't be a favorite food everyone eats, or her clothes, in case your big sister swaps with her."

My gut clenched. I tried to think of one thing and my mind went blank. What if I couldn't find something that would work?

The *traiteur* gave another little wave with her hand. "Don't worry about figuring it out. I promise that the right things will come to you. After you find each item, you'll attach it to one of the knots in the string. A different item for each knot."

I nodded slowly, my brain already whirring as I tried to think of my mamma's favorite things that only she loved or owned.

"Keep each thing in its own knot, and don't ever remove them."

The healing spell was getting more complicated. So many steps, so many things to remember. But then, Mamma had the hardest condition in the world to cure.

"What do I do after I tie in all the items?" I asked.

"I want you to find a memory for each knot next."

"How do I tie a memory? The string's not long enough."

The *traiteur* laughed. "You don't tie the memories into the string, Livie. I want you to cast your mind back to remember all the good things you love about your mother and all the good things she does for you."

I licked my lips. "What if I don't have any good ones?"

"You'll remember, but it's okay if you have a memory that you want to get rid of. Remember the good and let go of the bad. Cherish the happy ones and let the sad and angry ones disappear. Can you do that?"

I nodded and whispered, "Yes." It was gonna be hard, but I was willing to try. I wondered if this was what my daddy meant when he told me to try harder to love and understand Mamma.

Miz Allemond took my hands in her palms. Her fingers were strong and warm and I liked how she made me feel. "The last step is the most important and powerful of all. The only other thing this cure needs is your own special faith, Miss Livie Mouton. Faith. Do you know what that is?"

I'd heard about faith, but I wasn't sure I'd ever had any, or if I did, if I knew how to put it to use.

"Faith is God's power to move mountains with only a grain of mustard seed. A mustard seed is one of the tiniest seeds in the world. So all you need is that tiny seed of faith, Livie—and we're not trying to move a mountain, just wake up your mamma! Much simpler, wouldn't you agree?"

I bit at my lips and tried to nod. Waking up Mamma seemed like moving a mountain to me.

"Do you think you can give the healing spell all the faith you got inside you?"

Her black eyes across the table held me, not letting me glance away. Faith sounded simple and yet so hard. How could I know it really existed or if I was using it right? I think I needed a whole bag of mustard seeds! One for everybody in my family, and about a hundred for me.

"But the sleeping sickness seems so permanent, like there's no hope at all," I finally said.

"You gotta remember that with faith, nothing is impossible," Miz Allemond whispered, her voice so gentle I felt a sting in the back of my throat. "Herbs and treatments and *traiteur* skills are good . . . everything in my black bag, but oh, Livie, even I have to exercise my faith with every healing spell I do. It's the one ingredient I can't gather in the swamp or purchase in a store. But I do know that faith can start out as nothing and then grow to fill your whole soul. So can love. Love and faith go hand in hand; they always do."

"What do you mean?" I whispered.

"No matter what happened in the past, I know you love your mamma."

"But I always loved my daddy more. And that's a sin, ain't it?"

Miz Allemond shook her head. "Just because you got a special bond with someone, don't mean you don't love the other people in your family! Livie, child, you gotta find the love you have buried deep inside that's meant for your mamma. It's there. It's just been lost a while. And some lost things—well! They can take a whole lot of looking!"

I stared down at the yellow string with its nine simple knots. Closing my fingers around it, I felt something surge inside my heart. I'd do everything Miz Allemond instructed me to do. I didn't want to let Daddy down, or Mamma, or myself anymore.

"Now you leave that string on your Mamma's ankle. Don't take it off for nothing. Don't let nobody else touch it, neither. By the time that string falls off, your mamma will be healed."

Mamma *healed*. Mamma *awake*. It would take a miracle.

Well, that's what I was counting on.

Chapter 10

"I GOT MORE SCARED THE LONGER YOU WERE IN there," Jeannie said, holding T-Baby while I poled home. "Didn't know whether she'd put a spell on you or drowned you in the swamp out her back door."

The rain had stopped, but a puddle of rainwater on the pirogue seat was seeping through the old patch in my jeans. Mamma always said I was hard on my clothes. Maybe I'd have to break down and dig out those new jeans with the store-bought creases from my dresser.

I thought about what I'd just done. I'd visited the *traiteur* all by myself. Faye and Crickett, or my cousin Thibodaux, could never have done that. I almost couldn't believe it myself.

"So what happened?" Jeannie demanded.

It didn't seem like there were words to explain what had happened inside Miz Allemond's house or about the healing spell she'd given me. "She was nice."

Jeannie looked at me like I'd gone crazy. "Nice?"

"Yep, she was. And she gave me a healing to do."

"What is it? Besides a potato for warts, I never heard or seen nothing else."

"Well, it's sort of — sort of private."

Jeannie's face fell and I knew she felt left out, but I wanted to keep all the words Miz Allemond had told me inside my heart and think about them. Think about planting my mustard seed of faith inside my soul so I could have faith that the healing spell and God could bring Mamma back to us. An idea filled my head, just as the sun came out from behind the rain clouds. I think those mustard seeds of faith could help me grow into a better, more loving daughter and sister. I had an inkling that's what Miz Allemond was trying to tell me.

"It if works, I'll tell you all about it. Promise. Cross my heart."

Jeannie folded her arms across her chest. "Cross your heart, hope to die? Stick a needle in your eye?"

I laughed, realizing I felt better. What if I hadn't gone inside the *traiteur*'s house? What if I'd given up and gone home? I'd still be stuck where I was two hours ago. But now I had a plan.

"Hey, look at this, Livie," Jeannie said, picking up a broken tooth from T-Baby that had fallen to the bottom of the pirogue.

"I guess baby alligators need the tooth fairy to come visit, too."

"My daddy says alligator teeth are good luck."

I tucked the tiny white tooth, sharp and pointed on one end, into my pocket. I'd keep it safe until I figured out what to use it for. One thing I did know, I could use all the good luck I could get!

When we got back to the cypress cove, I slid T-Baby back under the elephant ears. He swam in happy circles; his beady eyes rising to the surface to peek at me as I untangled the strings of Spanish moss Miz Allemond had given me.

"I'll make a necklace, too," Jeannie said, although she had no idea what it would be for.

I laid the moss across my knees and began to braid the strands into a necklace. The clouds had blown away and the sun was beating down in huge, hot strokes. By the time Jeannie and I finished, we were sweating bullets. I tied three braided strings together into one long necklace and slipped my head through.

"I gotta drop you off now, Jeannie. Miz Allemond said I had to do this next part by myself."

"Can I watch?"

"Guess so." Miz Allemond didn't say I had to shoo everybody away, although it was embarrassing to have an audience.

My audience grew bigger. Crickett and Thibodaux were playing catch, and Faye was reading a book in the shade, and Daddy was boiling crawfish in the big vat.

I closed my eyes, trying to ignore the aching in my arms from all the poling I'd done as well as trying to ignore my watching family. Digging into the mud, I turned the boat in a circle.

The whole family stared as I maneuvered the pirogue in ten backward circles. After a few circles, the wake grew big and frothy. The pirogue rolled from side to side, nearly tipping me into the water, but I hung on for dear life.

Sitting on the dock, Thibodaux started laughing at me, but I didn't say a single word. I was proud of myself for not letting that dopey boy bother me. After I finished, I poled to the dock, tied the rope with my left hand around the piling, and looped it to the left just as Miz Allemond had told me to do.

Crickett raced down to the dock. "Where you been?"

"Nowheres. It's a secret."

Crickett clapped her hands. "I love secrets."

"This secret is only mine," I told her, crawling out of the boat.

Daddy came over and put a hand to my forehead. "You feeling all right, Sugar Bee?"

"Sure thing, Daddy."

"What was you doing out there on the water?"

"Nothing. Just practicing my rowing. Just for fun."

He gave me a sideways look and scratched his chin. "Thought maybe the sun had given you a fever and I had to call the doctor."

That night I pinched my arm a hundred times to stay awake. When I was sure Crickett was asleep, I stole out from under the sheets and tiptoed to the kitchen.

At the doorway I stopped. Aunt Colleen was kneeling on the floor beside Mamma's bed. She was muttering to herself, and I couldn't figure out what the heck she was doing. Then she lifted a strand of red rosary beads and kissed them in her fist.

I'd never seen Aunt Colleen praying before. How often did she do it? Praying at Mamma's bedside meant Aunt Colleen was worried, more than she let on, which made that awful, scared feeling rise up in my stomach. My aunt usually had a schedule in hand and no time for nonsense. Now her hair fell across her eyes like a wilted curtain as she bowed her head. Seeing her kneeling on the floor in her bathrobe and murmuring over her rosary made my heart twist inside my chest. She looked exposed and vulnerable but determined, too.

I glanced down at the knotted string in my hand and back to my aunt's rosary necklace dangling with a cross, a new thought trickling into my head. The two were similar in many ways. A rosary was a fist full of beads and a prayer for each one. I had a knotted string that would soon be filled with Mamma's personal "beads" as I searched for those mysterious good memories.

Maybe that rosary was Aunt Colleen's healing spell. Maybe my aunt wasn't scared so much as she was growing her own faith. Maybe she was asking God to help her wake Mamma up. If she could work on her faith, then I could, too. It was time to start putting the healing spell together.

My aunt crossed herself, then rose to her feet, knees creaking as she struggled to a standing position, one hand holding the back of a chair. She made her way down the hall and into the bathroom. Light spilled out, and then the door closed.

Shadows flickered everywhere. The living room windows were open, and a breeze blew through the screens.

I could hear the oaks rustling and our boats bobbing down at the dock.

From the hospital bed, Mamma's chest was rising and falling with even breaths. Aunt Colleen would be back quick, so I grabbed a flashlight out of a kitchen drawer and crept silently out of the house.

I'd finally figured out a few things to tie into the knots and it was time to start gathering them. Things my mamma used, things she loved. Nine of them! Could I figure out what to use so I could get the string finished quick?

I ran across the yard to the little art studio Daddy had built at the corner of the property. The cottage was painted lemon-cake yellow with big wide windows around each of the four sides. Mamma said good light was what an artist needed most.

Usually Mamma didn't let anybody in while she was in the middle of creation. She hung a cowbell on the doorknob so the family would know she couldn't be disturbed, but most of the time Mamma didn't care if we came poking around to look at the new paintings or to sit and talk while she mixed colors or cut the mats. Only I didn't do that so much, mostly Faye and Crickett.

The door to the cottage wasn't locked, but I hadn't been inside for a long time. Long before Mamma went to the hospital. Fact is, I couldn't remember the last time I'd come here. Mamma being an artist was another one of those girly things.

The porch was dirty, leaves and grass crunching under my bare feet. Cobwebs swayed in the moonlight, filling up the corners of the eaves. Tomorrow, I vowed, I'd get the broom from wherever Crickett had left it and finally clean up out here like I'd wanted to. Wash the rain-spattered, filmy windows, too. Mamma wouldn't be able to see very good through the glass if they weren't washed soon.

Inside, the main room was a big clutter. Mamma didn't have much use for housecleaning. She and Aunt Colleen had opposite personalities when it came to that.

Mamma always said she'd rather sketch on the banks of the bayou instead of wash floors. Funny how she wanted me to "act like a lady" but then didn't much care if her house was perfectly clean. One of those motherly contradictions.

The cottage was just big enough for a table, a chair, two easels, and a cupboard to hold supplies.

I switched on the flashlight, picking up the room's particulars in the beam's glow. Jars of paints spread out across the worktable. A palette still sat there, dried out, left from the day of the accident. A couple of old canning jars held brushes, every different size imaginable, as well as piles of colored pencils and charcoal.

Paint-splotched newspapers lay in messy heaps across the floor, and pictures cut out from magazines had been taped on the walls. I didn't know whether they were meant for inspiration or decoration.

Canvases stood propped against the walls in various stages of completion, mostly empty or prepped with primer. Paw Paw and Mémère had several framed paintings Mamma had done hanging at their house, and I remembered Mamma mailing off a picture to Aunt Colleen for a Christmas present last year.

Mamma was best at animals and landscapes. Over the years, she'd captured all the critters that lived around our house. A nutria swimming full speed downstream. A heron's nest filled with eggs, one cracked and ready to hatch. A snowy white egret soaring above the cypress. Pink azaleas blooming near the porch steps.

One of the easels sat empty, but the second easel held the painting Mamma must have been working on before the accident. I stepped closer and saw that it was half finished—and instantly my legs turned to Jell-O. The picture was of *me*.

Mamma had painted me standing in my pirogue, a pole clenched in my fists as I made my way down the bayou. Cypress trees draped with Spanish moss fluttered like there was a breeze inside the canvas. Coffee-colored water rippled from the bow of the boat. The colors, the motion—it all looked so *real*.

I reached out a hand, and then pulled back, staring at myself.

Mamma had painted me in green shorts, a yellow striped shirt, and bare feet. My usual tangled hair was coming loose from a braid, soft and wispy. Mamma had painted my face from the side, and I looked serious, like I was thinking about something very important, but there was a hint of a smile, too. My profile stared straight ahead, but that part of the canvas was still empty. I wondered where I was supposed to be going.

Dizziness rolled through the pit of my stomach. I was dying to know what Mamma had planned to paint, but the picture was like a puzzle with only a few clues. When I looked at the girl Mamma had painted, it was like a different me inside that canvas. I looked strong and determined and like I knew where I was going in life. All my life, I thought Mamma just saw me as a thorn in her side, stubborn and wild and contrary. We always pulled in the opposite direction, like two paddles turning a boat in a circle and getting nowhere. I never knew Mamma saw me like this. It was downright spooky. Like someone watching me without me knowing it.

A lump grew in my throat. This was the first time Mamma had ever painted a portrait of someone and she'd picked me first. Not Faye, not Crickett, but *me*.

At the worktable, I found a bowl of paintbrushes. The brushes were something that only Mamma used, and they fit exactly what Miz Allemond had told me to find. It was a perfect item for the healing spell.

I set down the flashlight, steadying it on the table so the light glowed onto the ceiling and I could see what I was doing. Carefully, I pulled out one of the long hairs that made up the soft bristles. Then I took the string off my wrist and tied the black bristle into the first knot and said a quick prayer. I pretended I was actually talking to God as if He was in the same room with me. It felt more real, not just a bunch of phrases somebody else wrote and I repeated.

When I finished, I picked up the flashlight and secured the door of the cottage, then ran for the house, almost falling over the rosemary bush at the cottage gate. A sprig of rosemary would be perfect for one of the knots! In the darkness, I could just make out the flowering purple blooms. I broke off a little piece and tied it into the next knot, then scurried up the back steps.

Tiptoeing into the kitchen, I put the flashlight back in its drawer and closed it tight again.

From the hallway came the sound of a toilet flushing. The bathroom door opened, the light clicked off, and I leaped as fast as I could into the galerie. I'd barely squeezed myself into bed around Crickett's sprawled form when Aunt Colleen stepped inside.

I held perfectly still and made myself look like I was asleep as my aunt swished around the bed. My heart pounded as I thought about what I'd just been doing.

Aunt Colleen whispered, "You awake, Livie? Crickett?"

I stayed silent, squeezing my eyes shut, and a moment later, she shuffled back to the kitchen. That was a close one. I pushed Crickett's legs to her side of the mattress, then got up to hide the knotted string in the top drawer of my dresser.

A shaft of moonlight fell across the bureau, lighting up my collection of frogs and alligators. A tiny frog with emerald glass eyes had fallen over and I righted it, making a circle with the other five. I'd have to look for a baby gator to add to the collection in honor of T-Baby.

Last year Faye had given me a handblown glass frog—on a necklace. And she knew I never wore jewelry so that necklace sat next to my collection not doing much. Maybe I should just toss out the silver chain and place the glass frog with the tiny green bumps with the others because I knew I'd never wear that necklace. She should have known better than to buy me jewelry.

I heard the faint strain of music drifting through the open windows. It was Daddy down at the dock playing his harmonica.

The sad songs made my throat ache. After a while I couldn't lie still any longer just listening through the screens. I wanted to be down there with him, curled up on the dock and watching the moon rise above the cypress. Jumping out of bed, I leaped over the porch steps and landed in the grass. I'd probably get red bug bites on my legs, but right then I didn't care.

"What are you doing out of bed, Sugar Bee?" Daddy said when I came up behind him.

"Heard you playing."

"Sorry I woke you."

"I wasn't asleep yet."

"You should have been sawing logs hours ago."

"That music is too sad for sleeping."

"Well, scoot on back to bed, Sugar Bee."

"Aren't you going to bed, Daddy?"

"Eventually. Just need some time to myself first. Then maybe I'll get my fishing pole, sit in my boat, and watch the sun come up."

"Can I go, too?" I asked, trying not to sound whiny.

"Not this time, Livie girl. Now get on back to bed."

Daddy gave me a little push up the grass. It seemed like he was trying to get rid of me. Today I'd done the bravest thing I'd ever done in my life going to see Miz Allemond, and I'd gotten closer to my mamma than I ever had before seeing that painting she was working on in the art cottage. Then I'd tied the paintbrush bristle into the string to start the healing magic and even talked to God, but I couldn't tell anybody a single thing about it.

"'Night," Daddy said, not letting me stay.

I stalked off to the house, my throat swelling up thick and hot. When he began playing the harmonica again, I yelled over my shoulder, "Can't very well sleep with all that racket, can I?"

Abruptly, the music stopped, and I bit my lips. Why did I yell at him to stop? I loved my daddy's playing. What was wrong with me?

Hot tears rolled into my mouth, and I hoped all my prayers for Mamma hadn't just come undone. As soon as I tried to do something good, I canceled it all out by snapping at my father. Maybe I was selfish wanting him all to myself. To pay attention to me when I didn't really deserve it, especially since I pushed Thibodaux into the bayou. Every day I just messed up all over again and made things worse.

"Please, God," I said, feeling a wave of misery crash over me. "Please don't erase the candle at the church today. Or the knotted string. Or the paintbrush and rosemary. Or the praying I was trying so hard to learn how to do. I made it to the swamp and Miz Allemond. Doesn't that count for something?"

I tried to swallow past the tears filling up my throat, but all I could hear in my head were the words I'd just yelled.

A moment later, my daddy jumped into his boat and pushed off from the dock. As if he wanted to get away from me.

Chapter 11

AUNT COLLEEN EYED FAYE AT THE BREAKFAST table the next morning. "You going to change your mind about this wedding?"

Faye stopped buttering her toast and a flush rose up her neck. "No, ma'am. Travis and me want to get married on July fourth when he gets his leave."

"Do you have a wedding dress?"

"Thought I'd try on Mamma's dress in her hope chest and see if it fits. We're about the same size as when she married Daddy."

"That's a fact, but don't you think every girl needs her own wedding dress?"

Faye's eyes grew big.

"Would you rather shop in Lafayette or Baton Rouge?" Aunt Colleen added casually. "We might even find something in New Iberia. That isn't as far to drive."

Faye started to laugh. "Don't matter to me, Aunt Colleen. Going shopping! For my very own wedding dress. That'd be heavenly."

Crickett had been licking the bacon grease off her plate. "I wanna go wedding shopping, too! Please, please!"

Aunt Colleen said, "It's up to Faye."

"Why, sure, you can come along with us, Crickett," Faye said. "It's not every day I get to buy a wedding dress."

"Will we have lunch at a restaurant?" Crickett asked.

Aunt Colleen smiled at her. "We have to eat, don't we?"

Thibodaux rolled his eyes. "I'm not going."

Crickett giggled. "Boys don't go wedding shopping, silly."

"What about Mamma?" Faye asked and I could see disappointment flare in her eyes, as if she was afraid she'd have to give the trip up as fast as she'd received it.

Aunt Colleen started filling the sink with water and soap, humming tunelessly as if she was pondering Faye's question real hard. I knew she was waiting for someone to volunteer to stay with Mamma, and it was obvious who she was waiting for. Like Mamma used to say, I wasn't born yesterday.

Frankly, I was mad Faye was going to get married and leave us alone in the first place. Not that I planned on missing her or anything. Give me a calendar and I'd mark the days left myself.

"I'll stay home," I finally muttered.

Faye's face lit up like a hundred-watt lightbulb. "You sure?"

I shrugged and tried to hide my terror in a forkful of eggs. "'Course I'm sure. Why not?"

"That's very generous of you to give up a day shopping to tend to your mamma," Aunt Colleen said.

I tried to finish my breakfast, but the scrambled eggs wouldn't go down. I pushed my plate away. "Daddy will be home, right?"

"Yes, he and I talked about it before you got up. Rosemary's having a peaceful morning and I already did her exercises so there shouldn't be any problems while we're gone," Aunt Colleen said. "We'd better get this show on the road, because the Fourth of July is creeping up on us faster than lunch."

After my aunt and sisters were gone, I sat on the floor, my back against the wall between the kitchen and the front room. I could keep one eye on Mamma and the other eye on the screen door, watching Daddy and Thibodaux fixing nets.

I studied my mother as she lay so still, the IV slowly dripping, the sheets tucked tight around her legs, and my stomach hurt even though I hadn't eaten anything bad. My eyes burned from no sleep. I'd tossed and turned, worrying over yelling at Daddy and how he didn't want to be around me. I thought and thought about the other seven items I still had to find. Most days it felt like I was hauling a cast-iron griddle around my neck, just like Aunt Colleen suspected. Spooky how she knew that.

I looked up just as a lock of Mamma's long brown hair slipped off the pillow. Letting out a cry, I scrambled to my knees, but Mamma's hair had fallen from the side of her face all on its own. She hadn't actually moved.

"Don't do that, Mamma," I said in a low voice. "Don't scare me like that."

"Who you talking to?" Thibodaux said, bursting into the house. He had a spade in one hand and a can of earthworms in the other.

"It ain't against the law for me to talk to my own mamma," I said stiffly.

He chomped down on an apple, his mouth chewing wide and noisy. "Never seen you do it before."

"You ain't so smart, T-Boy."

"I know what I see."

I didn't like him looking at me as if he had the whole situation all figured out. "Why don't you just shut up?"

Thibodaux shrugged and spit the apple core into the trash can. "Suit yourself. Just came to tell you we're going fishing."

"No," I said, racing to the back door, hoping my cousin was lying.

Daddy was on the steps gathering his tackle box. "Gonna check the traps and get some fish for supper, Sugar Bee."

"Can't I go with you?" The desire to go fishing with him made me ache with a physical pain. Besides, he was supposed to stay home in case Mamma needed him— in case I needed him.

Daddy's sun-darkened skin made the lines on his face deepen into beautiful trenches. "You need to stay with Mamma. We can't never leave her alone. You know that, honey."

"But—"

Daddy briefly touched my cheek. "You can do it, Sugar Bee. I trust you."

If something happened to Mamma, I had no idea what I'd do. She could fall off the bed or have a seizure, and I'd be too terrified to help her. I reached out and grabbed Daddy's arm. I knew he shouldn't trust me, but he didn't know that.

He patted my hand. "We gotta teach T-Boy to become a fisherman. He ain't never been bayou fishing. All that lake and stream fishing up in Montana — he don't know the real thing at all! We're just goin' 'round that first bend, so if you holler really loud from the dock I can hear you and come back if you need me."

They clomped down the back steps, and I broke into a sweat. I lurked about the living room, listening to Mamma breathe. I opened the curtains and moved the chairs. Then I wiped my fingers along the dusty mantle where the figure of the Virgin Mary sat next to the cross of Jesus.

I'd light another candle for Mamma, that's what I'd do. I found a book of matches and lit one, touching the flame to the double candelabra.

The phone rang. The sound startled me so bad, I actually yelped. Right when I did, Mamma gave a twitch. I stared at her. Had Mamma heard me scream? Was that a sign that her brain was still working? I was tempted to yell again just to test it, but decided I'd better answer the phone. By the time I got it, there was only a dial tone.

Quickly, I dialed the Martin house, hoping it had been Jeannie, but the phone just rang and rang and rang.

Then I remembered that I wasn't supposed to light candles in the house without Daddy's permission, so I blew out the flame and watched the smoke circle toward the ceiling.

It seemed impossible that a person could lie in a bed for so many hours, so many days on end. Why couldn't Mamma just open her eyes and sit up? Mamma *wasn't* dead. She didn't even look that bad hurt. The bandage around her head grew smaller all the time, the gash with its ugly line of black stitches shrinking every day, but somehow Mamma's brain was hurt so bad she was in a sleep that might go on forever.

I fell into the armchair. There was a hole in the side where the soft stuffing was falling out. I poked my finger inside, staring at Mamma's profile, the straight nose with the little bump at the top, her sunken cheekbones, the dip where her eyes closed.

Looking at her without anybody else around made my breath catch. Tears started to spill down my face, so

I pressed my eyes into my knees to get them to stop. Then somebody touched my arm and I screamed like a banshee.

It was Jeannie. "You're jumpier than beans on a hot skillet."

I batted a hand across my eyes to hide the tears. "Hey, I called you."

"I called you, too, then decided to just come on over." Jeannie made a face. "You don't look so good."

I tried to smile, but I felt like I was about to burst into a hundred pieces. "I think I'm going to hell." The words popped out before I could stop them.

Jeannie's eyes widened. "What're you talking about?"

The sentences came out in jerks. "It's—true. I'm the one that hurt Mamma."

"But my mamma said it was an accident. Your mamma fell—or something."

A trickle of sweat ran down my neck. "I'm the only one who knows." Speaking the words surprised me, and I wondered if I'd been wishing all along that I could tell her. I had to tell someone. If I didn't, I'd need someone to cart me to the loony bin in Shreveport.

"Your lip's bleeding," Jeannie said.

I touched my lip and tasted blood. That made me think about Mamma and the red swirls in the water, a picture I'd never forget as long as I lived. "If my daddy finds out he'll hate me and take me to the police. Promise you won't say anything."

"I'm sure it was an accident," Jeannie whispered, but I wondered if that's what she really thought, or if she said it just to make me feel better.

Before I could say another word, Mamma's head started flopping back and forth on her pillow. Her arms and legs began to twitch. A thin line of saliva snaked its way down her cheek.

"Livie, do something!" Jeannie shrieked.

What did the flopping and drooling mean? Was my mamma dying right in front of my eyes that very second? She couldn't die, not while I was here alone with only Jeannie.

"Please, Mamma, please stop!" I screamed.

Then Jeannie started screaming, too.

I ran around the hospital bed, afraid to get any closer, but scared to death Mamma would fall off the bed onto the floor.

"What do I do?" I moaned.

Jeannie stared at me, her eyes wild and frightened. "I don't know, Livie! Should I call my mother?"

I was trying to find where I'd put the phone when the screen door cracked, and Thibodaux started yanking at my arm.

"Shut up!" he yelled, and his red hair and freckles snapped me back to reality. "We could hear you all the way down the bayou."

Daddy came tearing through the door, and I was never so glad to see him in my entire life. He put his hands on both sides of Mamma's head and calmed the flopping. It was a miracle the way those hands worked. He wiped the drool away with the corner of his shirt and bent his head close. "Rosemary, bébé, it's all right, just relax."

His voice was as soothing as a hot bath; it was a wonder Mamma didn't wake up right then and there and wrap her arms around his neck.

"You children go on outside," he said. "She'll be all right."

I couldn't move, but T-Boy grabbed my arm and pulled me through the galerie to the yard. It was blistering hot in the sun. I was sure my skin would pop out with boils any second.

"Quit starin' at me!" I shouted.

Thibodaux acted like he didn't hear me. His eyes were as big as half-dollars. His head swiveled up and down, gawking like I was a freak show.

I stuck my hands on my hips and glared at him. "I said go away!"

"There's something wrong with you," he said, ignoring my orders.

I wanted to cram a sock down his throat.

"I've seen you touching and petting that alligator from the smelly swamp just like it was a baby." Thibodaux's voice was creepy. "You can pet it and hold it. Maybe you even kiss it, but you can't even touch your own mamma."

"I can so," I retorted, this close to telling him to take a hike where the sun don't shine. "You don't know nothing."

"I got eyes, don't I?" he said, sounding just like Aunt Colleen.

"Yeah, and them eyes are blind and should mind their own business."

"What if Uncle J.B. didn't make it back in time?" Thibodaux went on. "What would you have done, stand there and scream like an idiot?"

"She's not an idiot," Jeannie said in my defense.

Thibodaux rolled his eyes. "You weren't much better."

"Come on, Livie, let's go," my friend told me.

"Gladly," I said. We linked arms and started sauntering down to the dock to look for T-Baby, but I could feel my cousin's eyes boring into my back.

"I think you would have let her die," he said in a low voice, like he had to get the last word.

Without looking back, I said, "Seems like you're asking for another bayou dunking, Thibodaux Benoit."

He just snickered, and I kept my face straight ahead, my eyes blurring so I could hardly see where I was walking. I heard the back door open and bang shut and I knew he had gone back in the house, but my throat was raw, and my chest ached.

I wondered if T-Boy was right. I'd almost killed my mamma the day of the accident. Now would I let her die on that hospital bed just because I didn't have the courage to touch her? But what if I tried to help her, and she died anyway? Either way, I'd lose her forever.

I had no answers, and no direction, except for that healing string.

Chapter 12

I FOUND AN OLD SCHOOL NOTEBOOK, WHICH
was mostly empty, and sharpened a pencil. I figured I'd
write down any memories I could think of as I was
searching for the items to tie into the healing string. My
goal was to put it on Mamma tonight. It had to be
tonight. Time was running out.

Earlier, Aunt Colleen had shooed us all out of the
house when one of the doctors came to see Mamma's
progress. I sneaked back through the galerie and listened
at the kitchen door.

The doctor's voice was pleasant but to the point.
"Mrs. Benoit, you're doing an excellent job here in dif-
ficult circumstances, but I'm sorry not to see Mrs.
Mouton making much progress."

"Coma patients are tricky," Aunt Colleen said.
"And each person is different in their depth of unaware-
ness or when they begin to wake up again and come
back to us."

The doctor nodded. "The gash is healing nicely, and I see you took out the stitches."

"They were ready to fall out themselves." There was a pause and then I heard Aunt Colleen ask quietly, "What about her prognosis, Doctor? You know that's why I asked you out here for a special visit. Which I sure do appreciate," she added.

My chest squeezed up as I sucked in my breath. Aunt Colleen asked the doctor to come out and examine Mamma? I didn't know whether to be glad or suspicious.

"We never considered the coma would last this long," he answered, his voice dropping so that I had to strain my ears to hear. "We hoped that being here under her family's care would begin to wake her up, even in small spurts. Sometimes I've wondered if some coma patients purposely stay asleep to avoid something in their lives."

"What in the world are you talking about, Doctor?" Aunt Colleen huffed. "As if Rosemary can control the coma? That's ridiculous!"

"Just a theory," the doctor added quickly. "There's so much about the brain's activity we don't know."

Aunt Colleen gave a sigh. "Where do you recommend we go from here? Can we get a second round of tests for her?"

"I can order a CAT scan, perhaps an EEG, to determine the brain activity levels. But she needs to be at the hospital, of course. We'll have to readmit her."

I could hear my aunt pacing the carpet. "My brother-in-law needs to approve any tests. Or moving my sister from here."

There was silence, and then the doctor said, "I'll call him when I get back to the hospital and see when we can schedule the tests. I still think you need to take her to a nursing home. The burden on the family can be debilitating, and a nursing facility with rehabilitation experts has nurses 'round the clock."

"I'm fully aware," Aunt Colleen said. "We'll speak again soon then. Thank you for coming by on your way out of town. I appreciate your calling me back and making arrangements."

Seemed like my aunt had some sort of agenda to get the doctors on her side and get Mamma back into a hospital so *she* could go back home to Montana, but I wasn't sure. I guess there's a limit to vacation time. And Faye was getting married real, real soon. But I also thought it was strange that the doctor came by while Daddy was gone to town getting parts to fix the motor for his boat.

I stepped into the living room and saw that Aunt Colleen was now napping in the armchair next to Mamma. Daddy was fixing his skiff in the shed, T-Boy and Crickett were running for tools, and Faye was on the phone at the kitchen table with the wedding florist, her back to me.

Clutching the notebook, I kept on going into the hallway, heading to my parents' bedroom. I was so used to hanging out in doorways that I had to stop and just gaze at my mamma's room before I went inside.

The bed was unmade, rumpled with sheets, Daddy's clothes lying in small heaps all over, a stack of folded clean ones on top of a chair waiting to be put away. His smell lingered on the duffel bag he packed for his shifts at the faraway oil rig, sitting in the corner. A musty bayou scent wafted up from a pair of work boots hanging out of the closet, along with a whiff of shaving cream and boot oil from the adjoining bathroom.

With Mamma's clothes tucked out of sight into drawers and closets, her sewing corner untouched for two months now, it was like she had gone away for a visit to another country and missed her flight back. I guess she *was* gone—to a different place in her own mind. And the passport had run out, so she was stuck and couldn't get back. It occurred to me that I could be her passport, to bring her back to her *real* life, with the healing string.

Faye's voice chattered in the distance and I heard Aunt Colleen give a faint snore from the corner of the living room, so I stepped inside and cracked the curtains. A shaft of sun broke through, lighting up the room.

As I walked past the door to the bathroom and breathed in the smell of shampoo and toothpaste, I got my first idea. Mamma's perfume. I could use that on one of the knots. She'd worn the same cologne since high school, and Daddy got her a fresh bottle every year for her birthday.

I laid the knotted healing string on the counter, searching the medicine cabinet and bathroom drawers until I found the bottle of Prince Matchabelli perfume. As soon as I picked it up, I could smell the flowery fragrance. I poured a little bit into the cap and carefully dipped the middle knot into the liquid. Checking on the security of the knots around the paintbrush bristle and the twig of rosemary, I whispered, "Three down, six to go."

I spied Mamma's hairbrush lying on the counter beside the box of makeup Faye used on her. Carefully, I pulled one of the strands of Mamma's golden brown hair out of the brush and tied it into another knot. This was getting interesting. I felt like I was on a treasure hunt without a map but knowing I'd recognize the treasure when I saw it.

Treasure made me instantly think of Mamma's jewelry box.

I hurried across the room to her bureau, seeing myself in the mirror like a shadow in the late afternoon dusk. My eyes looked excited and jumpy as I cracked open the jewelry box, staring at the necklaces and earrings and trying to figure out what would work. Everything was too big and bulky to put into a single knot. Then I spied a small plastic envelope holding two ivory buttons. I recognized them from when Faye had tried on Mamma's old wedding dress a couple of months ago before the coma. Before Aunt Colleen took her shopping for her own dress. The back of Mamma's wedding dress had a row of these same ivory buttons. I found a spool of ivory-colored thread from the sewing table and cut a length to put through the buttons and affixed them to the healing string. Perfect.

There was something else in the jewelry box that would also work. An item that belonged only to Mamma—her broken crucifix chain. The links were small and delicate and tied right into one of the knots easy peasy.

I wandered to the closet and opened it up, staring at Mamma's pants and blouses and dresses hanging there in a silent row. Sandals and sneakers and a pair of black dress shoes lay in a jumble across the hardwood floor. Was there something here I could use? I certainly couldn't tie Mamma's favorite dress, the one she wore when she and Daddy went to Mulate's for crawfish étouffée and dancing, into a knot on a string.

The spool of ivory thread and the scissors gave me an idea. I ran for the scissors and back again to the closet, pulling out the dress and turning it inside out. A stray thread hung below the hem. I snipped it off and tied it into another knot, smiling with a sudden, warm pleasure.

Only two knots left. And the last two items came to me quick as a gator slurping silently down a bank into the water. I pictured my mamma trailing her hand in the purple hyacinth every time she went out in a boat. I'd tie in one of those pretty petals as soon as I could get down to the water.

I gave a satisfied sigh. The last knot could use some

luck, I thought, a good luck charm — and T-Baby's tooth had broken off the other day. Everybody knew an alligator tooth brought good wishes and good luck. Instead of carrying it around in my pocket to get lost in the wash, I'd tie the tiny tooth into the last knot on the string.

Now for the memory book. Sitting on the edge of the bed, I opened it up to a clean page and wrote down the numbers one through nine.

"What are you doing in Mamma's bedroom?" a voice asked from the doorway.

I jumped, startled and guilty.

It was Faye, hands on her hips, staring at me. Her foot tapped the floor as if she was impatient.

"Nothing," I said, standing up so quickly my pencil fell and rolled under the bed. "Now see what you made me do." I got down on my hands and knees to find the pencil.

"What *I* made you do? You're the one sneaking around the house."

Grabbing the pencil, I sat back up. "I'm not sneaking around. I came in here to look at some stuff."

"There's nothing in here that you need, Livie. Now go find something useful to do."

"You aren't my boss."

"Well, you need one."

"Nobody assigned you to it, so just leave me alone." Why couldn't she have stayed on the phone for another ten minutes? I was almost done. Actually, I had my items; I just needed to start writing down good memories—if they existed. "You're making me lose my concentration," I told Faye, giving her a glare like she often did to me and which my older sister had perfected to an art form.

She laughed, and I felt my teeth grind. "Your concentration, huh? So what have you got hidden in your hands behind that notebook?"

I pressed the spiral notebook against my chest and backed away from her. The string was tucked between that and my shirt, and there was no way I was going to let her see it. "None of your business. Now leave me alone."

"Not until you get out of here and go do something responsible. Go on!"

"I hate you bugging me all the time," I cried, wanting to bop her over the head with something, but there was nothing very useful within reach, and if I used the notebook she'd see the knotted string with all the beautiful items I'd found.

Slowly, I backed out of the room, keeping my face toward her so she couldn't reach out and grab me or pull the notebook out of my hands.

"Oh, Lord, Livie, you drive a person crazy!" Faye said, marching into the hall after me and firmly shutting the master bedroom door. "I could care less about what you have."

"A minute ago you were dying to see it," I retorted, and then I stuck my tongue out at her and raced for my galerie bedroom, slamming the door between me and the kitchen and locking it.

I sank onto my bed, barely breathing as I waited to see what she'd do. Five whole minutes passed before I lowered the notebook to my lap. Looked like she wasn't going to chase me down. I was safe for the moment.

I stared through the windows, watching a breeze ruffle through the cypress, swaying the grayish green moss and rippling the surface of the bayou, and racked my brain trying to come up with at least one good memory.

Well, I sure wasn't getting very far. Maybe I was right and Mamma and me didn't have any good memories at all. Maybe I didn't even *own* any faith or love seeds to sprout, let alone grow.

While I waited for my brain to kick into gear, I ran down the back steps to the pier, checking first to make sure I was alone. The coast was clear. Reaching past the elephant ears, I picked a purple hyacinth flower, making sure there was enough stem for tying. The flower would fade soon and shrivel up, but I didn't think that mattered.

Racing back to my room, I carefully slipped the hyacinth into the empty knot reserved for it and smiled, feeling a catch in the back of my throat as I looked at the entire thing all completed and pretty.

I'd done it. I'd found the perfect items, and I couldn't help but love the healing string just a little as I stared at some of Mamma's favorite things.

Touching the nine-knotted strand as I studied the various items, an idea slowly came into my mind. The thread tying the ivory buttons into one of the knots and the thread from Mamma's favorite dress made me think about sewing and needles. I got up and opened my bottom drawer where I kept my jeans. I hadn't worn any for a while because it was too hot now and I strictly wore shorts during the summer, but I had a pair that used to have a hole ripped in the knee. Actually, several pairs, and Mamma had sewn up the holes with her needle or put a patch in. I closed my eyes, remembering her sitting in the lamplight, her eyes going cross-eyed as she threaded the needle with dark blue thread. That was something Mamma had done for me. I guess it was a good memory and showed she cared. At least she cared about my jeans. That was probably close enough to caring about me since they were my favorite jeans.

I wrote the memory down in the number-one spot on the page.

This memory thing was going to be hard. I'd have to think some more. Meanwhile, I'd get the healing string tied on Mamma while I kept searching.

While Crickett was taking a bath after supper, and I was sitting on my bed in my pajamas, I knew another hard part was yet to come.

One by one, my family went to bed, the lights turned out, and I pretended to read a book as I leaned against my pillow. After another hour, Crickett finally stopped kicking and fell asleep. I yawned and kept waiting.

When the house quieted down, I stood up, slipped the healing string into my hand, and crept through the kitchen door. I was lucky. Aunt Colleen was taking a shower and Daddy was locking up outside. I only had a few minutes, and it was taking all the guts I had to step closer to the hospital bed.

My mouth was dry as I stood in the shadowy front room and studied Mamma's toenails. They'd been painted a pale pink. Faye's doing. My eyes moved up along Mamma's legs to her hands. Her fingernails were done in the same pink color.

The water shut off down the hall. Sounded like Aunt Colleen was done with her shower.

My heart pushed into my throat as I lifted the corner of Mamma's nightgown with shaky fingers. The knotted string was growing sweaty in my other hand. I held both ends out in a straight line, positioning the string underneath Mamma's ankle. Quickly, I looped it around and tied a double knot, managing to do the whole task without touching her.

Letting out my breath, I folded the nightgown back over Mamma's ankle so the string didn't show. I hoped Aunt Colleen wouldn't take it off and throw it away when it was time to give Mamma her sponge bath. Hopefully, she'd know it was special, just like her rosary.

Chapter 13

A THWACK, THWACK, THWACKING SOUND WOKE
me up a few days later. Harsh sunlight hit me square
in the face. I bolted upright. Crickett was gone, pillow
on the floor, sheets balled up in the middle of the bed.
I could tell it was much later than I usually slept.
Sleeping so long made me feel disoriented and groggy,
and it was so darn hot, I was already sweating.

I jammed my legs into a pair of shorts, threw a shirt
over my head, and ran out the back door to find out
what the noise was. In sixty seconds, I was grabbing
chunks of my uneven hair to twist into a thick braid to
get it off my neck. I was sure I looked like a Mack truck
had run over my head.

Daddy had the ax from the shed and was whacking
at the old cypress stump he'd ripped out of the bayou
mud. The stump had dried out now and would make
good firewood for next winter.

T-Boy watched Daddy work, hands on his hips, his eyes moving with each swing of the blade.

Daddy's arm muscles bulged, his shirt stained with sweat. He worked feverishly, the deep lines on his forehead knotted together like rope.

I took a step backward, knocking my shoulder into the porch post. Daddy was hacking the stump clear to smithereens, as though he'd have liked to kill it. That wasn't firewood he was making.

T-Boy gave a holler of satisfaction, completely unaware that what was happening was anything but normal. I had a horrible feeling my daddy was losing his mind. Mamma's coma was making everybody crazy, not just me.

I wiped my palms on my shorts and all I could think was that my daddy was going off the deep end. When he paused to wipe his brow, Miz Allemond's words ran through my mind for the hundredth time, like a rat on a wheel.

Wood pieces, like shotgun shrapnel, lay all over the yard. An even stranger thing happened next. Daddy began arranging the chopped-up sticks and kindling into one huge, messy heap. T-Boy ran around the yard, gathering up the pieces to build the pile even higher.

I shook my head. My cousin was completely clueless.

Then Daddy knelt on the grass, pulling a box of matches from his pocket. He struck one across the flint, and held it under the slivers of kindling. It took a couple of tries, but soon tiny blue and yellow flames began licking at the wood. A minute later, the flames just died right out. Daddy frowned and then picked up a container of kerosene and sprinkled it over the entire pile of chopped-up wood.

He lit another match and tried again. This time the old cypress caught hold of that fire and one small flame turned into a hundred. Within another fifteen minutes, the fire was roaring, the smoke turning into a sash of black ribbon curling over the bayou. The heat got so strong I could feel it clear up on the porch.

This was the craziest thing I'd ever seen. Burn perfectly good wood, especially after all the hard work of hauling the stump out of the bayou mud?

"Go around the side of the house and get the hose, just in case we need it," I heard him tell Thibodaux.

Crickett came up from the bank and helped Thibodaux unwind the garden hose. Daddy looked tired and old, more like Paw Paw every day. He stared at the flames, and I would have given anything to know what he was thinking.

Suddenly, Faye came up from behind and put her hands on my shoulders. Our eyes met, and I glanced away, feeling self-conscious because we rarely touched. Right now, I wished she'd reach out and hug me more than anything. I wanted to cry on her shoulder, pretend she was Mamma, and have her tell me for sure everything was going to be all right. The not knowing was killing me. Holding the secret in was eating up my insides, like termites gnawing at the underbelly of a house.

Did Faye think Mamma would get better? Did she think Daddy's behavior was bizarre? Did she hate it when Thibodaux poked Mamma's legs or breathed on her face?

After a while, the flames began to die out and the fire became a bed of hot, sizzling coals.

"Why'd Daddy burn that woodpile just now?" Faye asked. "In fact, I've been wondering what made him pull up that stump in the first place."

My shoulders twitched as her hands stroked my back. I liked it and I didn't want her to stop. She was starting to remind me of Mamma more all the time. She had the same long fingers, the same way Mamma used to look at me from under her eyelids. For some reason it didn't bug me like it used to. I'd give anything for Mamma to open her eyes up for real and look me straight in the soul.

I shrugged. "He always said he would someday."

"Yeah, but why now?" Faye dropped her hands and leaned over the porch railing. I could feel her eyes following me as I climbed up to sit on the railing, as if she was trying to dissect me like a frog in science class. "Livie, I gotta tell you something," she suddenly said, her voice turning serious.

My heart began to thud inside my chest. I braced myself for bad news.

Faye bit at her lips. "I'm thinking that maybe I should call off the wedding."

I gulped, not sure I'd heard her right. Faye rarely ever confided in me. "You mean give Travis his ring back?"

Tears filled my sister's eyes and she brushed a hand across her face. "Aunt Colleen said she's gonna go back to Montana after I get married next week, and there won't be anyone to take care of Mamma. Her leave from the hospital will be over, and I think Thibodaux misses his daddy, too."

My cousin said all the time how much he hated it here. Only time he seemed happy was when he was fishing or doing stuff with Daddy, and I never thought about him missing his father in the Veterans Hospital. I sort of figured T-Boy's daddy couldn't walk or talk right. That he was crazy as a loony bird.

"But Daddy's here to take care of Mamma," I told her.

"He can't do that all day and all night and bring food home, too. You know that, Livie. You're old enough

to start stepping up to the plate. But I know you won't."
She shook her head, her face red, her nose running.
"Which means I can't get married. Not yet. Maybe not
never. Oh, I don't know!" Faye began to cry harder,
turning away from me so I couldn't see her.

"But—" I was so shocked, I didn't know what to
say. I couldn't imagine Faye without Travis or Travis
without Faye. They'd been friends their whole lives and
ever since they were fifteen they said they wanted to get
married. "But you have to get married. It's all planned.
Maybe Aunt Colleen can quit her job and live with us
all the time."

Faye snorted. "Sometimes, Livie, you seem so dense.
Aunt Colleen isn't going to leave her husband in
Montana. Her home is there. Maybe you're just as self-
ish as I've been thinking."

My eyes filled at her words. That hurt. Hadn't I been
cleaning around the house, keeping watch over Mamma's
art cottage, and trying not to fight? Now I turned away
from her, hiding my tears.

Faye grabbed my arm and made me look at her. "You ain't the only one hurting, you know."

I squirmed under her gaze. "Never said I was."

"Oh, but you act like it, Livie. You surely do act like it."

"You don't know everything," I told her, feeling the secret ready to burst through my chest. What would she say if I told her the truth about that day and Mamma's accident? I was so tempted, the words ready to rush out of my mouth, but I already knew the answer. She'd hate me forever and so would everybody else.

"It's up to you, Livie. The only way I can get married is if you start helping with Mamma. You have to bathe her and dress her. I know you're capable; you just don't want to. You just want to go off playing in the bayou with your pirogue. Bringing home a batch of crawfish once in a while ain't nearly enough. And it'll kill Daddy if he has to do it all. That's what Aunt Colleen said. The strain would do him in. I'm not sure he's had a full night's sleep in two months."

There was a roaring in my ears, louder than the raging fire had been, louder than a motorboat speeding through the narrow bayou, louder than a Category 5 hurricane. Aunt Colleen said Daddy could die from all the stress and worry over Mamma? Fear seized me, and sweat poured down my neck. Gripping the splintered wood of the porch railing, I stared at the ground. "I don't know what to do, Faye. I'm scared of her. If I touch her, I might make her die!"

"Don't you think we're all afraid of that, too?" Faye began to cry again, and I could feel the aching sound of her sobs right in the center of my chest.

"But Aunt Colleen thinks I'm killing Daddy," I whispered, barely able to say the words. "Do you think that, too? Do y'all think that?"

"No, Livie, we don't. But we all gotta pitch in and help. Work together. You don't seem to understand that."

I jumped off the porch and ran into the galerie, throwing myself on the bed and burying my face in my pillow.

My sister followed me, and the bed jiggled as she knelt on the spread beside me. "Livie Marie Mouton, what is going on inside that head of yours?"

"I think you all just hate me," I said, my voice muffled because I couldn't look at her.

I felt her hand press onto my arm. "Why in the world would we hate you?"

"Because I'm keeping Mamma in the coma. Because it's all my fault. Because I don't help. I'm sure you can come up with another ten reasons."

Faye sighed. "I'm sure I could, but I'm not going to. I'm tired of being mad at you, too. Tired of no sleep. Tired of not knowing what's going to happen. Tired of being so scared." Softly, she added, "Is that how you feel, too?"

I was so surprised to hear her say that, it took me a moment to answer. Then I nodded, my face still hidden in the hot pillow.

The bed creaked as she shifted her position and came closer. "Hey, I'm getting married soon. At least, I hope I am. Can we declare a truce?"

I finally lifted my head an inch and gave a little shrug. "Okay."

"Can I give you a hug, or is that against the law?" Faye asked.

I nodded but didn't move. She leaned down and hugged me from the back, brushing a hand against my hair. I lay stiffly, not knowing how to hug her back, and then she left.

Chapter 14

THE SMELL OF PANCAKES AND CANE SYRUP HUNG in the air the next morning.

The house was dead quiet as I pulled on my shorts. Seemed like I'd slept through breakfast again.

I glanced out the window. Faye was hanging fresh laundry on the line and listening to the radio. Crickett and T-Boy were playing down at the dock, splashing each other with water. The air in the house was stifling and it was one hundred percent sticky muggy, so I felt grouchy and out of sorts.

When I walked into the kitchen to get some corn-flakes, the voices of Daddy and Aunt Colleen were loud in the front room.

"J.B., we can't do anything else for her. You need to take her back to the hospital. Or find a nursing home that can care for her."

"They can't do nothing," I heard my daddy say.

"Rosemary gets 'round-the-clock care right here in her own home. With people who love her."

Aunt Colleen sighed. "It takes more than love to bring someone back from a coma. People here are getting tired. Faye's getting married in a week. Then she's gone. Gone for good. Do you understand what that means? Even if she says she'll come back and help once in a while, she needs to go on with her own life as Travis's wife. And Olivia—well, that girl won't go anywhere near her mother. Have you noticed, J.B.?"

My heart began to pound, and I strained to hear what Daddy replied, but he only mumbled.

"I've tried all the techniques I know," Aunt Colleen went on in her calm nurse voice. "We've talked to Rosemary, sung to her, stimulated her senses, her muscles. I even tried some—well, some stronger methods a couple times."

"What's that?" Daddy asked sharply.

"Don't get alarmed," Aunt Colleen said smoothly. "Techniques used for coma patients. Things that will— well, things that might help *shock* Rosemary into waking up. Like putting ice cubes on her bare skin. Pricking her feet with a needle."

"I won't have you torturing her!" I heard Daddy pace the floor, breathing hard, but then he spoke again, like he was hoping for a miracle, too. "Rosemary do anything after these shock treatments?"

"Not a thing, J.B. I hoped. Oh, Lord, I hoped."

"We can't give up. She still eating, ain't she?"

"Only IVs, but she's wasting away, getting so thin."

The floorboards creaked, and I started inching toward the back porch.

"J.B., you've got to prepare yourself. Rosemary is not coming around. The longer it goes, the less likely she'll ever come out of it. Have you thought about the possibility that she might be permanently brain damaged? That skull fracture, bleeding on the brain. Even if she woke up, she might not be the same Rosemary we've always known."

"Don't matter to me," Daddy said stubbornly. "I'll always love her."

"Of course you'll always love her, but I'm trying to

be realistic here. You have to face facts. You just might have to let her go."

Something crashed to the floor, and my heart nearly jumped out of my chest. I peeked around the kitchen corner, only to see that Daddy had slammed his chair to the floor.

"I won't never let her go!" he said.

I crossed the kitchen in two leaps and slammed the screen door behind me. Escape, that's all I wanted. My heart was going to swell up and bust and bleed all over just like Mamma's head had done. I'd hurt Daddy. I'd hurt everyone.

I stood at the bottom of the steps, gasping in hot sticky air, when an arm slipped around my shoulder.

It was Faye. "Hot day, ain't it?"

I nodded, my heart pounding in my ears. "Aunt Colleen — Daddy —"

"They arguing about Mamma again?" Faye asked. "They do that every few days. Surprised you never heard it before."

"Aunt Colleen makes it sound so scary."

"It *is* scary," Faye said, leading me around to the front porch where it was cooler under the oaks. "I feel scared to death all the time. Just like we talked about yesterday."

I'd been thinking about that conversation, too. I'd run into the galerie and thrown myself on the bed, leaving her crying on the porch, but Faye had followed me and talked to me. She'd hugged me, wanting to make peace. I was secretly glad and pleased that she'd made the first move. Made it easier for me to stop avoiding her. I thought about all those times I'd run away and hid out in my room or the bayou, and I knew I hadn't been very nice.

"It's nice to have you not glaring at me all the time," I said now.

She laughed as she sat on the top step of the porch facing the road. "Sometimes I wish so bad you'd confide in me, Livie. But I've always had to be extra long-suffering around you."

"Well, I gotta be extra patient with you, too," I told her, slowly sitting down beside her.

She snorted at that. "Guess we're even then." It was quiet for a moment and then Faye said, "I have noticed you've been doing extra chores around the house. The other day when I talked to Father John about the wedding ceremony, he told me you'd been in to see him and to pray for Mamma. That made me real glad, Livie, but why didn't you tell anyone?"

"I didn't think anybody would care what I did or where I went."

A single tear started to slip down Faye's cheek. "Seeing you keep Mamma's art cottage cleaned up and helping in the kitchen and hearing you went to church for her helps me forgive you a little bit."

I felt tears start to fall down my face as well, and I wondered what else she was going to tell me. I knew, suddenly, that I needed to forgive her, too, for all those times she'd yelled at me to leave her alone when her girl-friends were spending the night, or to quit sneaking her fresh-baked cookies when she'd made them for a special occasion. 'Course, she could have shared and not been so selfish. Or *told* me she'd baked them special. She didn't have to yell and glare and tell me to get lost like I was an annoying bug.

Faye glanced at me out of the corner of her eye. "I almost called you a Miss Priss when I saw you'd cut your hair and were wearing a ribbon. I wondered what that new girl had done with the old Livie."

"I think she's locked up in the closet. At least for an hour here and there."

Faye gave me a tentative smile and I tried to smile back, even though my mouth felt stiff. I did think about how nice it was sitting there in the shade, the two of us, for the first time, although I was nervous not knowing where our conversation was going to lead.

"Tell me what you're thinking right now, Livie," Faye said. "Right this very second."

I swallowed. "You really want to know?"

"I do."

"You won't laugh or say it's stupid?"

Faye hugged her knees and shook her head. "I promise I won't do that ever again."

"Well, um, I was thinking that for the first time we're sitting here talking like we're real sisters instead of enemies."

"Sometimes, Livie, you make me feel ashamed. You're right. I haven't been so nice at times, but now, I'm going to treat you more like a grown-up. I brought you out here to let you know that I've made my decision. I'm going to call Travis tonight and cancel the wedding. Aunt Colleen can't stay forever, and heaven knows not even you and Daddy can probably do it alone. Even if you did try to help more."

"But if you cancel the wedding you'll think that's my fault, too! You'll just hate me all over again."

"I'm working real hard not to hate you, little sister," Faye said. "Actually, I love you even though you drive me crazy."

"I love you, too, even though you drive *me* crazy," I told her.

She let out a small whoop. "Sometimes you're so honest and then other times I think you're keeping some kind of big, awful secret."

I held my breath, my scalp prickling, hoping she wouldn't go on. "But Travis—the wedding—you mean you wouldn't never marry him?"

She studied her feet, the chipped red polish that needed redoing, and lifted a shoulder. "Probably just postpone it or something. Thing is—we never know when Mamma will wake up."

The pain in my chest returned in full force. "God won't make her stay like this forever, will He?"

"That's the whole thing, ain't it? He could let Mamma stay in a coma for years. Or she could end up dying after all."

"Don't say that!" I told her. I didn't want to hear her give up. I was trying so hard to inch forward and believe, to have faith in myself, in the healing spell, in Mamma, and trying to sprout those small seeds.

The screen door squeaked, and Daddy's boots clumped across the porch boards. Without a word, he sat down between us and I scooted over to make room. "You girls forgive me for eavesdropping?"

"'Course, Daddy," Faye said.

I closed my eyes, feeling the warmth of my daddy's arm around my shoulders.

"We only got a week until there's gonna be a wedding at our house," Daddy went on, and I could feel the deep rumble of his voice inside my chest as he talked over my head. "Invitations are out. And I hear the bride and groom love each other and want to spend the rest of their lives together."

"Oh, Daddy," Faye whispered.

"I know you're feeling guilty for leaving us here with Mamma," Daddy went on. "And I couldn't have done all these long weeks without you, Faye, that's for sure. All you girls been so strong and helped without a single complaint."

"It's not fair for me to leave," Faye said. "Mamma needs so much help."

Daddy nodded. "That's true, but you got your own life to live, honey. Never expected you to stay out here caring for Mamma the rest of your life. Rosemary is my responsibility. Twenty years ago, we promised to care for each other no matter what happened. Just like you and Travis will promise yourselves to each other forever."

"But—"

Daddy put up a hand. "Nope, don't want to hear it. The wedding is on. Travis only has those few days' leave so we can't even postpone it. And it's gonna be a happy day for you, darlin'. We all gonna put our smiles on. I know Mamma would want it so. When she wakes up she'll want to see your wedding album, and we can't be looking sad and teary-eyed."

"Oh, Daddy," Faye said again, but instead of weeping she gave a laugh as Daddy made his face all mopey and sad to try to get us to smile.

He gave Faye a kiss on the forehead, and then he turned and kissed me on top of my hair. I felt his lips trembling, and right then I knew why I loved him so much. Daddy was scared, too, but he had faith in Mamma, in her getting well, and in our family.

Sitting beside my sister and my daddy made me realize that faith wasn't something a person could hold in their hands or tie into a healing string. It was something

I had to believe and hold in my heart, even if my heart seemed broken. Daddy believed Mamma was going to wake up and look at wedding pictures one day — despite Aunt Colleen's and the doctors' predictions.

Were faith and love entwined together somehow, like all of Mamma's belongings I'd twisted into the knots of the healing string? I felt a sudden whoosh of understanding and gladness. That was it. That knotted string was helping me mend all the broken pieces of my heart back together.

The next week, Faye dragged me to the linen closet. She unfolded one of Mamma's quilts. "Think this will stand out good enough?"

The blanket had bloodred roses outlined in tiny stitches and a yellow scalloped border. It was so fancy Mamma had always saved it for best company. Since best company hadn't shown up yet, she'd never even washed it. It was as bright and vivid as the day she quilted it.

I helped Faye hang the blanket over the railing of the back porch and then we tied crepe-paper wedding bells along the railings, stringing them out in a long, pretty row.

I ran down the lawn to make sure everything was hanging straight. The wedding bells swung in the breeze, making the house look like a party was just around the corner.

"Can you see the quilt okay?" Faye called.

"Yep, just like a rose garden."

When the wedding guests paddled down the bayou, they would see the quilt and know they were at the right place. Faye had also hung a second quilt on the porch facing the road so people driving from town could spot the wedding house.

The last few days had been nothing but work, work, work. Aunt Colleen and Faye worked me until I was bone tired. We cleaned the house, pulled weeds, mowed the grass, scrubbed windows, polished the silver, and dusted Mamma's good china. Daddy took Faye into town to shop for food even though most guests would bring a dish to contribute to the potluck supper, and I helped pull up two hundred pounds of crawfish from the traps to boil.

The evening before the wedding, Travis showed up on our doorstep, coming straight to our house from Mississippi as fast as he could drive.

He was taller than I remembered and wearing his navy "blues," as he called his casual uniform, not taking the time to change, he wanted to see Faye so bad. His face was razored so close, his skin was smooth as a baby's and pink from slapping cologne on it.

"You smell good," Crickett told him, putting her hands against his cheeks and leaning in close to sniff.

"Better than engine grease?"

"Much better," Crickett said with a nod.

I kept staring at his haircut. He had a new buzz cut and he looked like a big kid with his ears sticking out from his head.

Travis caught me watching him. "Do I meet with your approval, Miss Livie Mouton?"

I shrugged, trying to hold back a smile. "I guess you'll do."

"We're going to be brother and sister, you know."

I blinked at him, realizing that fact for the first time. What a strange thing, to have a brother.

Travis took Faye's hands in both of his, grinning all the while. "I think she's speechless with astonishment."

"She's not sure if you're going to be an in-law or an outlaw," Faye told him.

"I'll put you on trial for the first year," I said, my face growing hot.

"Deal," Travis said, holding out his hand for me to shake. Then he and Faye strolled down the porch to sit in the swing together and talk and talk like they hadn't seen each other for a year, even though it had only been two months for boot camp.

In the deepening twilight, Daddy swept all the porches, and Crickett and I lugged out the ice coolers for drinks the next day. I wanted to listen in on Travis and Faye's mushy conversation but could never get close enough to understand a single word. I couldn't imagine what you'd say to a boy you were going to marry the very next day.

Later, before bedtime, Faye modeled her wedding dress for Crickett and me. She smoothed her hand down the satin and twisted her head to look at the short train gliding out behind her. "I just want it to be perfect."

Crickett reached out to touch the pearl beads. "I helped pick it out," she told me.

"You done a good job," I said.

Suddenly, Faye folded herself to the floor, the dress billowing around her in a balloon of lace and pearls. "Wish I knew I was doing the right thing leaving y'all for my honeymoon."

"You nervous about getting married?" I asked.

Faye shook her head. "Nope, just about Mamma. I'm worried folks'll say I'm being selfish."

"Aunt Colleen's going to stay another week, and I heard Daddy tell her he'd probably hire a private nurse for a few hours a day so he can work." I heard myself saying these things to reassure my sister even though she already knew them herself. Reassuring my big sister was something I'd never done before, and Faye looked at me with a thoughtful expression as if she was thinking the same thing.

I stared at her half-filled suitcase, clothes scattered around the room, her bureau and mirror and the movie posters pinned to the walls. Once summer was over, I was going to get her bedroom for my own. No more sharing with Crickett. No more feet kicking me in the middle of the night. I figured it would be heavenly, but I had a feeling it might get a little lonely, too.

Faye would never live here again, except as a visitor. I'd be the oldest girl in the house. Daddy was going to expect me to help care for Mamma, but how could I do that when I couldn't even touch her?

"Daddy can't go on forever with so little sleep," Faye said, rubbing a finger along the white satin hem. "I think he needs to hire a nurse, at least part-time, but don't know how he'll pay for it."

I lifted my shoulders. "Told Aunt Colleen it was his worry and nobody else's."

Faye sighed. "That sounds like Daddy."

Crickett was counting the beads on the wedding dress. "You got over a hundred pearls! Aren't you excited to see Travis? He's gonna be your *husband* tomorrow."

"Of course I'm excited! Don't he look different since boot camp?"

"I think he looks funny," I said. "His hair's so short he looks like a baby with big ears."

Crickett started giggling, and then she warned Faye in a grown-up voice, "You better not lay down in that dress, it's getting wrinkled."

Faye starting unhooking the front buttons. "You're right, bébé. I get to wear it all day tomorrow."

Daddy appeared in the doorway, leaning against the doorjamb, one hand rubbing his face, the other stuffed into his back pocket. Crickett jumped up into his arms and laid her head on his shoulder. He patted the back of her nightgown as he looked at Faye.

"You get a good night's sleep, now, you hear? I'll stay up with Mamma."

"I'll take my turn, Daddy. It's okay, I don't mind."

"Aunt Colleen is doing the second half of the night. You are going to be the prettiest bride on the whole bayou tomorrow. And that means no dark circles under your eyes."

Faye got up to give him a hug and her arms also went around Crickett, who was still sitting in Daddy's arms, her head against his shoulder. I watched the three of them together, a strange sadness sweeping over me. It was our last night at home together before Faye became Mrs. Travis Boudreaux.

I stayed on my spot on the floor just watching them, waiting for the inevitable feeling of being left out, of not being quite a part of my own family. I'd spent so much time the last couple of months in doorways and on the fringes of my own deserted island.

Leaning my head back against Faye's bed, I didn't feel so much like an outsider anymore. At least not like I used to. Was it because of the things I'd done to help Mamma? Maybe because Faye and I had talked for the first time like real people, not just sisters who fight and try to tolerate each other.

"I just wish Mamma could be part of it," Faye murmured against Daddy's shirt, and the sad hurt in her voice made my own throat ache.

"I'm sure she'll know her daughter's wedding is going on. Maybe she'll even wake up just in time for the 'I do's.'"

"That would be the best wedding present in the whole wide world," Faye said, burying her face in his shoulder.

"There, bébé," Daddy said, patting her. "Go to bed. Only sweet dreams tonight."

On my way through the front room, I stole a glance at Mamma's foot under the sheets like I did every night before going to bed. The string was still there, and I breathed a sigh of relief.

After I tied it on Mamma's ankle, I'd had a moment of panic the first time Aunt Colleen saw it. She'd been getting water and towels ready for Mamma's bath when she spotted the knotted twine. "Now what's this?"

I waited in the kitchen, holding my breath, praying my aunt wouldn't take a pair of scissors and slice it off.

Then I heard her say, "Must be Crickett's doing. Seems like I remember talk when I was a girl about strings that are supposed to cure babies."

The string was safe, but it was getting dirty now, although the knots were still tied. How long did it take a nine-knotted healing string to fall off and work? I was afraid that it might take months, years even.

Chapter 15

NEXT THING I KNEW FAYE WAS YELLING, "GET up, Livie, get up! It's my wedding day!"

My older sister came into the galerie and flopped into the middle of the bed between Crickett and me with a huge, happy sigh. "I'm getting married today. For real. To Travis Boudreaux."

Crickett put her arms around Faye's neck. "I'm going to miss you."

"Don't cry, honey," Faye said, kissing her. "Today is a happy day."

"I'm crying because I *am* happy."

"You're impossible," I said, tickling Crickett. "You cry when you're sad and you cry when you're happy. How we ever supposed to figure you out?"

All of a sudden, Faye reached over and wrapped her arms around me. "I'm going to miss you, too, Livie."

I lifted my chin up and down, feeling shy around her again. Missing Faye when she was married wasn't something I had thought much about, but it was starting to hit me. Her getting married was real, and it was permanent. After today, I'd hardly see her anymore. She was moving all the way to Mississippi. I wondered if it'd feel like she was my sister anymore, or if it'd feel more like she was just some old married person. I wondered if she'd change into someone different.

"I told Daddy this morning I'd be back for a month to help out when Travis goes to Virginia for training," Faye said. "You just gotta hang on for a while, okay?"

"Okay," I whispered, knowing that even one day was going to feel like a hundred, especially when Aunt Colleen left to go home to Montana. With a sudden intensity, I hugged her back, realizing that I didn't want Faye leaving us alone here. I wasn't ready to be the oldest sister around the house and have all that responsibility. I'd been just fine with letting her do it all. I guess we'd always been so busy being annoyed at each other, I hadn't appreciated her very much.

Faye sat up, her nightgown twisting around her hips. "Today I've got to get two people ready for the wedding," she said, not quite letting go of my hand. "I think this is probably the last quiet moment I'll have before this day goes crazy busy." She ticked the items off on her hands. "Extra-special makeup, Mamma's party dress. I'm taking a long soaking bath with bubbles, and then curling my hair with the hot rollers. Crickett, will you be in charge of the punch?"

"You gotta show me how."

"Just lime sherbet and 7-Up poured in the punch bowl. Easy as pie."

I spent the morning helping Daddy set up tables and chairs on the lawn and a wide canopy tent with tall poles to stake down for shade. Underneath we arranged tables for the gumbo, jambalaya, red beans, and boudin. For decorations, we hung red, white, and blue crepe paper and tied flags on each corner of the smaller guest tables. Last of all, Daddy set up two big steamers for boiling the crawfish.

Then Faye yelled that it was my turn for the shower.

"Leave your hair long," Crickett told me when I got out, a towel wrapped around my head in a turban like Mamma used to do. "And wear some lipstick like Faye."

"I'm not even twelve yet. What do I want with lipstick?"

"You'll be twelve next week," Crickett reminded me.

I'd be starting middle school this year, too. Mamma's plans for putting me in charm school seemed like a hundred years ago.

"I like getting fancy for Faye's wedding," Crickett added, jumping up and down on the bed.

"Well, don't get used to seeing me fancy," I told her. "Probably won't happen again until *you* get married."

Faye came out of her bedroom, bringing her box of makeup into the steamed-up bathroom. "You can wear some of that Pink Frost, Livie. Just a hint of color, but it'll make you look older." She winked at me and I stuck my tongue out at her. Then we both laughed.

I leaned into the bathroom mirror and tried on Faye's

lipstick. I looked like a clown so I rubbed it off and tried again. There, now at least it was straight. After cutting my hair and baking snickerdoodles last week, I couldn't make too many changes or I'd give my family a heart attack.

I let out a gasp as a memory rushed into my mind. The only reason I knew how to make snickerdoodles at all, my favorite cookie, was because Mamma had taught me once. When she was in a good mood, she'd make a batch, and she'd give me a whole plate to eat with milk while they were still warm.

Pulling out the notebook from my dresser drawer, I wrote it down before I forgot.

I shook off the towel turban, but before I could start on my hair, Faye tugged me into her room and sat me on the chair in front of the wall-length mirror.

"Let me do your hair today, okay? You don't mind?"

"I don't mind," I told her, secretly liking how she was paying attention to me.

"Sit back and relax," she said as she applied the conditioner and then combed out the wet tangles, her hands brushing against the skin of my neck. I remembered when I was younger and Mamma practically had to sit on me to keep me still so she could comb out the bath snarls. I'd end up crying and running out of the room. And yet, right now felt nice with Faye. Her hands reminded me of last summer when Mamma would braid my hair with her cool hands on a sweaty morning. A time when she was gentle and quiet and paid attention so I could get my hair out of the way and run outside to help Daddy sand the hull of his skiff. Hair combing was a combination of good and bad memories with Mamma.

Today, my older sister even looked like Mamma with her hair in fat curlers and pin curls on her cheeks and wearing a lace slip. As soon as I was finished dressing, I was going to write that good memory in my notebook, write down the bad one, and then cross it out with the pencil to get rid of it.

Faye pulled out a soft blue hair band and put it around my hair, fluffing out my bangs, which were now almost dry. She turned them under with Mamma's hairbrush to give them a little poof so they weren't so straight and boring.

"Can we use that green ribbon in the bottom drawer?" I suddenly asked.

Faye raised an eyebrow, and then pulled open the drawer. She exchanged the blue headband for the sea-green ribbon and nodded. "Green does look good on you. Do you like the rest of your hairstyle? It looks like one of those flips out of the beauty parlor magazines."

"Everyone will think you tied me up in the closet and brought out my evil twin."

"Even with fancy clothes on I guess you're still the same Livie we all know and love, but there's hope for you yet." She made a face at me.

I glanced at her in the mirror and our eyes met. "Is how I look right now what Mamma was always trying to do to me?"

Faye smiled softly. "Mamma was always just trying to pull out your own special beautiful. Now go get dressed. Paw Paw and Mémère will be here any second."

Faye had ironed my yellow Easter dress and I stepped

into it so I wouldn't ruin my hairdo and she zipped up the back. I leaned in closer to the mirror, trying to recognize myself, my breath fogging up the glass. I looked so peculiar, so *different*. Like a girl out of a play or a movie, not my own self at all.

A tingle scurried straight up from my stomach. Was this the girl who would be the oldest daughter in the house now? The girl who could take care of her mamma without running away to live in the swamp?

I rooted in my drawers and found a pair of white stockings. Then I dug into the closet for the shiny dress shoes Mamma had bought almost three months ago. Once I'd buckled them on and stood up, I realized that they pinched my toes like a red ant bite. Did my feet grow so fast, or were they just fat from going barefoot every day?

The glass frog necklace with the green eyes on top of the dresser caught my attention. Slowly, I picked it up and felt the silver chain glide across my palm. The tiny clasp was hard to open, but finally I got it around my neck and looked in the mirror. The green frog matched the green ribbon, as if they were meant to be worn together. For some reason, I looked complete now.

Quickly, my brain popped with a new memory. I grabbed for the notebook, because that little glass frog made me think about frogging with Daddy. Usually it wasn't my daddy that woke me up to go frogging at all. It was Mamma that came into my room at midnight, whispering kisses into my ear while Daddy got the boat ready and the gear.

Fast as I could, I wrote down the memory and scratched my ear, as if I could hear Mamma's voice right there, so close.

Faye came back through the door, searching for her missing hairbrush. She halted when I turned toward her. "You're wearing the necklace I gave you!"

I shrugged. "Seemed like the sort of day to put it on."

"Thank you, Livie. It's the perfect gesture for a day that's going to be perfect." She turned me around to face the mirror and her breath tickled my ear. "First time you get all dressed up, it feels mighty strange, but that pretty girl you see in the mirror was there all along; she just hadn't shown up until today."

"Weddings are a no shorts, no overalls, no braids, and no bare feet event," I said with a dramatic sigh. "I guess I can sacrifice a day every now and then."

The clothes felt strange on my body, the shoes uncomfortable, but that girl in the mirror was beginning to grow on me. I liked how Faye said I could be both kinds of girls. I didn't have to pick one over the other.

As soon as my older sister raced back inside to finish her makeup, the phone rang.

"Livie," Jeannie said, her voice loud in the receiver. "You won't believe this in a million years. I've got the chicken pox and I can't come to the wedding now."

"Chicken pox! You mean you never had it before?"

"Guess not. And my little brother has it, too. Mamma's gonna stick me in an oatmeal bath. Like I'm a little kid."

"My mamma did that, too, and it really helped." I realized that I was actually speaking out loud about a good memory. I'd had a bad case of chicken pox and I remembered how awful it itched. Mamma put me in a tub of oatmeal, which soothed my skin, and then she rubbed pink ointment on all the red spots. After I was in my pajamas, she spent the afternoon reading picture books aloud to me in her big bed and giving me raspberry tea.

My heart sank. "I can't believe you're gonna miss Faye's wedding."

"Me neither. I love weddings, and Faye's is going to be the best, but Mamma said we'll drop the wedding present off for Faye and Travis when I get better."

"Okay," I whispered, feeling dopey for being so disappointed, but I couldn't help it. Jeannie wouldn't see me in my new clothes and my new hairdo. I wondered if she would've even recognized me.

"I'll call the minute, no the *second*, I get rid of these spots, okay?"

I wanted to jump in my boat and pole up to Jeannie's house to see her, but I didn't have the luxury because two minutes later guests started arriving.

Travis Boudreaux was the youngest of fourteen children, so his parents were real old like Paw Paw. All his married brothers and sisters arrived with carloads of offspring. All those kids filled up the yard real quick.

"Where's my girl?" Travis asked, pulling my hair. He looked nice in his brand-spanking-new white navy uniform. The pants were creased sharp as a razor, as if he'd ironed them all morning.

"You can't see Faye before the wedding."

"But today *is* the wedding!" Travis roared, and then he swung me around like I was five instead of practically twelve. "There's Father John," Travis said, setting me down. "Think I'll go hurry things up."

The food table was getting loaded with casseroles and stews, dirty rice, shrimp and oyster platters, rolls, home-made breads, and my favorite, powdered-sugar beignets.

I reached out to sneak a bite of shrimp just as Paw Paw and Mémère's motorboat came down the bayou at full speed, Paw Paw whooping and hollering.

Whenever Mamma saw them coming she used to close her eyes and say a prayer. "One of these days, he's going to flip himself right into the bayou and swim with the alligators," she'd always add with a shake of her head.

"*Bonjour, ma cherie!*" Paw Paw boomed out.

"I'm coming," I yelled, running down the grass to the dock, Crickett right behind me.

"*Ma petite filles!*" Paw Paw said, sweeping us up into his arms. He pulled my hair ribbon. "Sure lookin' mighty bootiful, *shar*. Breakin' those boys' hearts, too, I bet."

I made a face, then helped him hook the ladder on the side of the boat so he could carry Mémère down to the dock. I held the ladder steady while he picked her up from her metal chair in the prow of the boat. She loved feeling the wind and spray on her face.

Once she was on the dock, I gave her a kiss, and she mumbled a few words out of the corner of her mouth, asking about Mamma and wanting to see her. The stroke my grandmamma'd had last year left the right side of her face droopy, like a pair of baggy underdrawers, and her right arm almost useless.

After Mémère had seen Mamma and talked to Faye,

she settled under the canopy with a cup of punch and a straw while Paw Paw tuned up his fiddle.

A second fiddler had come down from New Iberia, and the two of them were wrinkled as prunes and skinny as starved cats, but they were also the best fiddlers in the parish. Daddy was going to play his harmonica, and two more musicians had shown up to pound the drums and yammer on the accordion while people danced on the grass.

I sauntered back to the house, curious about what Mamma looked like. Nobody but Faye was in the house and she sat holding Mamma's hand. The satin and sparkly beads on my sister's wedding gown glowed in the slanting afternoon sunlight. Faye had fixed her hair in ringlets around her face and I'd never seen her look prettier.

"You look beautiful," I told Faye. "You really do."

"Thank you, Livie. Don't Mamma look nice, too?"

Faye had dressed Mamma in the party dress Daddy bought her last summer when he took her into New Iberia for dinner at a fancy restaurant for their anniversary.

The dress was a rosy-pink taffeta with an empire waist and a heart-shaped neckline. Today my sister had even fastened Mamma's own wedding pearls around her neck. Her hair had been washed and dried and now it curled in soft waves around her face.

The house was silent as I sat in a chair across from the hospital bed; one of the few times I'd gotten this close to Mamma. Outside, the guests were chattering, the band was warming up, and a car horn was honking, but it all seemed very far away.

My gut tightened when I thought about what I'd have to do once the wedding was over. I stuck a fist into my mouth, gnawing on my knuckles.

It was time for the miracle, I thought: Mamma waking up and walking outside to sit next to Daddy in the front row, and to watch him give Faye away. I squeezed my eyes shut and willed it to happen, wishing as hard as I could, but when I opened my eyes, Mamma was quiet as ever.

Taking a slow breath, I tried to think thoughts that were full of faith. I'd try to be patient a little longer and trust that God — or Miz Allemond — knew what they were doing.

Wait, maybe that wasn't how it worked. Perhaps He was waiting for me, testing me. I'd never thought of it like that before. Which made me wonder how long the test would last and if I was passing or not. I wanted to turn all those F's into A's, but I wasn't sure what else I needed to do.

"It's time to start," Faye said, rising. "I can hear Travis through the windows. Now where'd Aunt Colleen get to? I haven't seen her for hours."

The front door burst open as Aunt Colleen and Thibodaux rushed in, all dressed up in their Sunday best. Between the two of them, they carried a fat, round wedding cake. Three layers high with snowy white frosting. Miniature pink roses decorated the edges.

"Oh!" Faye stared at the gorgeous cake. Then she laughed. "I forgot to pick up the cake!"

"That's why I had to make an emergency run into town," Aunt Colleen said as she and T-Boy carried the cake to the kitchen table and set it down with a soft thump. "Whew!" Aunt Colleen wiped her brow with a gloved hand. She was even wearing a flowered hat on top of her long silver hair. "What would you do without me?" she added with a wink, but even I knew she was just teasing.

"I truly don't know," Faye said, hugging her. "Serve bread and water?"

I studied my aunt, thinking about all the times she gave that little wink and how it reminded me of Mamma. Like Easter Sunday when Mamma winked at me as we sat in the pew at church and listened to the music. I went into the galerie and wrote it down in the number-six spot, then hurried back to the kitchen.

"Now don't go messing up your hair and makeup," Aunt Colleen scolded, then put a hand to Faye's face. "I've never seen a more beautiful bride, honey. Your mamma would be so proud and happy."

Faye's eyes glistened and her voice caught as she said, "I kept hoping today would be the day Mamma woke up—"

"Shh, don't think that way, honey," Aunt Colleen told

her. "Won't do us any good, and tears'll just ruin that good makeup job."

When the band played the wedding march, I watched Faye walk slowly across the lawn holding her bouquet of roses and carnations. A smile lit up her face like the sun was shining directly on her, and she gazed at Travis, never taking her eyes off him.

The groom grinned like a cat that had swallowed a mouse. He'd always had a shy smile and a slow, easy way of speaking that made you feel comfortable and safe. He and Faye had been sweet on each other so long, maybe I could picture him as a big brother. It was like our family was growing instead of shrinking.

Daddy walked Faye up the center aisle, gave her a kiss on each cheek, and then stepped back by the window. He'd popped out the screen earlier and now he reached through to hold Mamma's hand during the ceremony.

When Father John pronounced Faye Sarah Mouton and Travis Alan Boudreaux husband and wife, I felt a wave of emotion deep down in my belly. Sweet and bitter at the same time. Maybe this was what Crickett meant when she said she cried when she was happy. I was happy for Faye because she was so joyful with Travis, but I was sad to lose her now that I'd just found her. And sad that the healing string hadn't worked fast enough. I kept wondering what else I needed to do besides thinking of the last three memories. Actually, I knew what I needed to do; I just wasn't ready yet. But I wanted to be! I wished it wasn't so hard and scary.

As Travis bent to kiss Faye on the lips, Crickett pinched my arm and giggled. They held the kiss for a long drawn-out moment and a cheer rose. Travis's brothers clapped and whistled and I felt a wave of heat rise up my face. I'd punch my husband if he did that to me.

"That was some kiss," Crickett whispered loudly, and everybody laughed.

Aunt Colleen cut the cake and everyone had two or three pieces before the dancing even started. Then the band began playing in earnest and it was just like a summer fais do-do, except Faye and Travis danced the first number inside the circle of guests while everybody watched and oohed and aahed.

I overheard people making comments. "What a handsome couple they make," and "May they be blessed with love and many children." Then Daddy danced with Faye, holding her close. After that, it was a free-for-all. Everybody danced with everybody else. Neighbors from down the bayou, grammas and granpas, daddies with their daughters, sons with their mammas.

As dusk descended, Daddy lit the lanterns. Stars sparkled like glitter. The cicadas buzzed, keeping time with Paw Paw's fiddle. Me and Crickett poured the band some punch when they took a break.

Thibodaux and the rest of Travis's little nephews and cousins gathered around Paw Paw's feet while he told them stories of alligators back when he was a gator hunter as a young daredevil.

I got myself a cup of slushy 7-Up punch and sat on a folding chair, listening with half an ear. I'd heard Paw Paw's stories my whole life. Tonight, every time I'd glanced in a mirror or saw my reflection in a window, I knew I looked different, but I also felt different. I wasn't part of the younger kids running around the yard, playing tag among the dancing grown-ups, but I also wasn't one of the teenagers making eyes at each other and flirting. I didn't feel out of place, just in between, like I was leaving childhood and about ready to step into a new doorway of life. I wasn't quite ready to go that far, so I contented myself with sitting back and watching my family and neighbors have a good time.

When I saw Faye a little while later, she was covered with money. Dozens of green bills had been stuffed into her sleeves and pinned to her satin bodice and up and down the long, trailing train.

"You're loaded," I told her. "And look at that stack of gifts on the table!"

"It's like Christmas," Crickett exclaimed. "Can I help you open them?"

"'Course, honey," Faye told her. "When Travis and I come back after our honeymoon we'll open all the presents together."

Gifts and Christmas reminded me of some easy memories. Mamma always made the holidays special, decorating the house and making lots of good things to eat. She was happy and sang carols and danced around the house with us. Why had I forgotten all these good things about Mamma? Why had I covered them all up with bad feelings and anger?

Just then, a rocket shot off into the sky, arching above the live oaks. It exploded into the air, shimmering with red sparks.

"Fireworks!" Crickett cried, clapping her hands.

Another one exploded with a shower of white. Then there were red, white, and blue ones for Independence Day, then green and orange, pink and yellow, booming across the bayou.

"They're beautiful," Faye murmured. I watched Travis put his arms around her waist as he bent to kiss her neck.

I glanced away, feeling funny watching them, but then I peeked back again, curiosity getting the better of me. I wondered what it would be like to be that in love with someone. Since I couldn't answer my own question, I went to go have another beignet and sausage. I'd just filled my plate and found a spot on the lawn when a tall, dark-haired boy walked up and sat down on the grass next to me. I looked up and stared into the eyes of T-Jacques Landry. I was so startled I swallowed a piece of sausage wrong and started coughing. T-Jacques thumped me on the back and then I took a gulp of punch.

"What are you doing here?" I managed to splutter.

"Been here the whole time with my folks," he said, pointing across the yard. "Hanging out by the cove. You look different tonight, Livie."

I could have said the same thing about him. I also felt my stomach jump in that strange way it did whenever T-Jacques was nearby. I hardly recognized him tonight. He seemed taller, like he'd grown three inches in the past month. And he was wearing nice clothes, the ball cap was gone, and his hair was slicked down.

Funny that he'd picked my favorite spot by the cove, too, the place where T-Baby lived. I'd been so wrapped up after the ceremony helping Crickett keep the punch bowl filled and taking away dirty dishes and cutting wedding cake that I hadn't even seen my alligator since the morning.

"You're wearing that ribbon, aren't you?" he asked, pointing at my hair.

"This ole green ribbon?"

"You were talking about it the day I saw you at the church."

He remembered that? I didn't know whether to be secretly pleased or to punch him for staring too close. T-Jacques looked bigger tonight, too, with muscles in his arms. Must be all that wood chopping. I could even smell him, some kind of boy smell I couldn't figure out, but it was nice, and I liked it, although I wasn't going to tell him that. But I found myself staring at his face and speculating if he'd slapped cologne on his skin.

"You live in the same place you used to when you're not at your summer camp?" I asked, trying not to think about how weird my life was getting. Faye's wedding day had me doing and thinking all kinds of strange things.

"Yep, down near Bayou Alligator about ten miles. You ever been there?"

I lifted my shoulders. "Maybe once or twice. You get lots of gators down there?"

"There was a nest across the water a few years back, but my daddy and uncles got the fish and game department to help 'em move it so we could swim without getting eaten."

He said it so matter-of-factly, I had to laugh. Then, speaking of gators, I wondered if I should show him T-Baby in the cove. I wondered what he'd think, if he'd scold me for keeping a baby alligator as a secret pet. 'Course, this was a boy who threw softballs into church windows, even if accidentally.

"Few weeks ago I built my little sisters a waterslide out of a piece of sheet metal," T-Jacques went on. "Tamped down the sharp edges and angled it on to a wooden stand so it's sturdy and slants just right."

"Really?" Now that was interesting. "I'll bet that's fun. Like a real swimming-pool slide."

"Yep, they whoop and holler all the way into the bayou. Splash me on the dock while I'm trying to work. You ought-a come visit sometime and try it out, go swimming with us."

I felt myself blush, picturing us doing cannonballs off the dock together. "I don't know about *that*."

"I run a garden hose up to the top of the slide and let it trickle down so it stays wet and Sissy, the five-year-old, don't get stuck. Plus the metal don't get so hot, either."

"I guess that'd work pretty good," I told him. Actually, I thought it was real clever.

T-Jacques glanced down at my plate. "You done eating?"

I shrugged. "Guess so."

"Let's dance, then."

"Oh, I never dance—" He grabbed my hand anyway and pulled me to my feet so fast I didn't have a chance to run away.

Within two seconds, T-Jacques had his arm around my waist and we were dancing to one of Paw Paw's slow ballads. His hair fell over his eyes, and he twirled me under the arch of his arm. I nearly fell over my own feet, but T-Jacques caught me and somehow we kept going. Once I tried to move away, but his arms tightened.

"Hey, if you're Cajun, you better learn how to dance."

"I prefer watching," I muttered.

"Time to stop watching, don't you think?" His gaze was so powerful, I had to glance away. My mind felt like it was speeding off without me, and I was scared and excited at the same time. Right now T-Jacques was looking at me like I was the prettiest girl at the wedding, and my thoughts went all twisty like a pretzel.

"We got something in common, you know," he said. "You're in the middle, ain't you?"

"Middle of what?"

"Your family. Your sisters."

I shrugged again. "So what?"

"I can just tell the way you hang back." He smiled again, a slow, knowing smile that made my stomach jump very annoyingly. "I got four older sisters and four younger sisters. All girls, 'cept one. Me."

"That's a lot of sisters to keep track of!"

"Most days they talk so much I can't get a word in edgewise, so I just go outside and fix the fence or bring up some catfish. Lots of times, nobody notices except when I come home for supper and eat half the gumbo and rice by myself."

"That big of a family, no wonder you gotta do so much wood chopping."

"You noticed, huh?" He looked pleased, and I wished I could snatch back my words.

I tried to wriggle away. "Just shut up, T-Jacques."

He stepped back. "Hey, no need to run away before the song is over."

I bit my lip, and then grudgingly started dancing again.

I thought about all the times I'd felt alone this summer, like I was on my own deserted island, hanging out in doorways, on the edge of my family instead of part of it. Seemed like T-Jacques felt the same way, and I wondered how he'd guessed the truth about me. T-Jacques noticed things, which was strange for a boy.

"I don't have any brothers, either," I said after a while. "Which means I'm the one that helps my daddy with the hunting and fishing."

As soon as I spoke, I wondered if T-Jacques only liked girls who dressed up and curled their hair, but then he smiled and I felt my guard come down a notch.

The music softened, coming to a close.

"Your family's been having a hard time lately," T-Jacques said quietly, dipping his head down so only I could hear.

His words made my eyes sting, and I was glad dusk was filling up the yard to hide my face.

"We should go fishing sometime before the summer's over," T-Jacques suggested. "I just made me a new crab trap."

My heart began to thump. "Well, I don't know about that," I said, even though I knew I'd love to see how he made his traps.

"I could show you some good places in the bayou."

That was tempting. I raised my eyes and T-Jacques was gazing straight at me. He was serious, not just teasing, and I knew he meant it. He was thoughtful, thinking about my mamma, which made me trust my instincts about him, but I wasn't sure how to agree to go without sounding too eager or too dopey. I tried to work out the words in my head and make them come out of my mouth, but they weren't assembling together very well, so I didn't say anything. Then Paw Paw sawed the last chord on his fiddle and let out a "yee-yi!" and everyone laughed.

My cheeks grew hot and I felt more and more tongue-tied the longer I went without responding. Quickly, I mumbled, "I have to go," and ran off for the safety of the food canopy.

My heart and mind were going a hundred different directions as I watched the circling couples and sipped another cup of punch. How did other girls manage talking to boys like it was as easy as breathing? I wasn't sure I'd taken a decent gulp of air in twenty minutes.

T-Jacques watched me from the other side of the yard, his arms folded across his chest. I started feeling bad that I'd walked off, but not bad enough to go talk to him — at least not yet. To go seek him out on my own was downright embarrassing, and I felt myself squirm just thinking about it.

On the last song, T-Jacques suddenly disappeared from view. I was sorry I didn't get the chance to say good-bye and I wondered if I'd insulted him.

I found myself looking for him in the deepening twilight, a twinge of disappointment rising in my throat. When I glanced backward one last time, T-Jacques surprised me by coming up behind me, taking my hand, and walking straight to the middle of the dance floor. We were locked in, surrounded by all the other dancers.

"Now you can't run away again," he said with a sly grin.

"Very tricky, T-Jacques."

We turned and then turned again and I could feel his eyes on my face. It was getting late now; even the crickets were slowing down and going to sleep. Frogs sang in the bayou, and a breeze ruffled the air.

"So you figure out yet if you're going fishing with me?" he asked. "I drive a boat real safe."

I laughed. "Maybe."

"I'll take that as a yes."

I saw Daddy put down his harmonica and head straight for us. T-Jacques tightened his grip on my hand and whispered, "I'll find your number and call you. We'll go early in the morning when the fog's hovering and the fish are biting."

"That's my favorite time of day," I said, and my hand flew to my mouth as I realized that it sounded like I'd just agreed to go with him.

"Cutting in," Daddy said to T-Jacques, twirling me away.

"Daddy!"

T-Jacques stepped back, hands on his hips, and I could feel his grin growing bigger as my words sank in.

"Don't worry, he'll be back," Daddy told me. "I

wanted to make sure I got a dance with my girl before the night's all gone."

"What makes you think I care about that T-Jacques Landry boy?"

Daddy gave me a smile that looked just a little bit sad. "Just one of those fatherly instincts. Meantime, I can see we need some dancing lessons before the summer is over."

"I got a better idea. You can teach me how to trap muskrats."

Daddy laughed and kissed the top of my head.

As he twirled me around the grassy dance floor, I thought about Mamma in her anniversary dress last summer when she and Daddy went out dancing at Mulate's. The same dress she was wearing right now for the wedding. A thread of that dress was knotted into the string, and I wondered if it made my daddy sad thinking about not being able to dance with her right now.

I remembered waving good-bye from the front porch as they left to go out on the town, but there would be no wedding memory of them swinging around the dance floor, or taking their turns with Faye and Travis. I could still picture Mamma's happy smile from a whole year ago when she held Daddy's hand as they walked to the truck, and Daddy opened the door for her, giving her a wink.

My forgotten memories and the threads of Mamma's rosy pink dress were all tied up together into that knotted healing string. This was a good memory and a sad one at the same time and my heart hurt inside my chest just thinking about it. As soon as I could, I needed to get my notebook out to write it down because it was a memory I knew I had to keep.

The storm that night started with the wind. I hadn't noticed the sky filling with black clouds because it was already dark, but after the dancing was over I realized that the stars were gone, blotted out by a buildup of black, boiling clouds.

Cups and plates started blowing off the tables. Families bundled up babies and picked up their empty dishes from the table. Cars loaded up; boats were tied loose from the dock. Faye kissed everybody good-bye and thanked them for coming.

I watched Travis packing his two-door Chevy with Faye's suitcase and makeup bag for their honeymoon in New Orleans. My heart gave a lurch. The wedding was over. Faye was really leaving. It was suddenly happening too fast.

The Landry family got in their skiff, a lantern on board to light the way back down the bayou. I pretended I was busy securing my pirogue, but I could see T-Jacques looking at me. When he lifted his hand in a wave just before the bend in the river, I kept my own hand clenched tight to my side, but that darn T-Jacques kept grinning anyway. Then I felt bad about not waving good-bye. Shoot, I'd see him again. There was no worry about that. And maybe I really would go fishing with him like I'd said.

I stood in the driveway next to Crickett as Daddy eyed Travis. "You promise to take care of my daughter, young man?"

"With my life," Travis told him solemnly, shaking hands.

Then Daddy hugged him hard and kissed his cheek just like he did everybody in the family.

Faye kissed Crickett over and over again, and Crickett, of course, was bawling. Then Faye hugged Aunt Colleen and Thibodaux and Daddy, who gazed into her eyes and nodded his head, as though assuring her that everything would be fine.

"You have a good time, and be safe," he told her, and Faye nodded, her eyes swimming with tears.

Last of all, Faye stepped over to me and engulfed me in her long, skinny arms. I gave a spurt of surprised laughter and felt sudden tears coming on. "I will see you very soon, Livie," she whispered in my ear.

I breathed in her perfume as her fancy-curled wedding hair tickled my face. I tried to say good-bye, but the words were locked inside a wedge of tears.

"You'll be okay," Faye added. "Remember the girl we saw in the mirror this morning. She's still a part of you, and she can be here whenever you need her to help you be strong."

"Okay," I whispered back, hoping she was right.

"And remember that Mamma needs you now. Needs you more than you realize. Talk to her, Livie. That's all you have to do right now. Just talk to her."

Travis helped Faye into the car and revved the engine, and then the whole family was waving and crying their good-byes, over and over, like we'd never see her again.

Travis's older brothers had tied tin cans to the bumper, and the empty cans rattled and bumped as they made their way down the road. Shaving cream in curlicues on the back window announced the news. *Just Married.*

The red taillights on the Chevy disappeared, and I felt a sudden, sharp loneliness squeezing my heart. Leaving home and Daddy and the bayou sounded awful to me, but Faye sure looked happy.

Aunt Colleen came out of the dusk, linking her arm with mine. My nose was running just a little, and I sniffed and leaned into her warm side as she put her arm around me.

"She's going to be missed, that's for sure," my aunt said softly.

"Uh-huh," I agreed, finding it hard to get the words out.

The wind began to whip my hair around my face. A clap of thunder burst overhead and a flurry of raindrops pelted the yard.

Crickett squealed and ran for the house. The wind picked up a tin bucket and rolled it across my path. I shoved it under the porch steps just as the trees began to bend, branches creaking as if they were going to snap in two.

The rain came harder, slapping my face and arms, making wet splotches across my dress, and stinging my bare legs. I thought about T-Jacques and hoped his family had made it home. The Landrys' hunting shack would be swaying like crazy in this storm. I pictured T-Jacques and his father holding up the paper-thin walls with their bare hands to keep it from falling over and I couldn't help smiling. He could put all those new muscles to work.

"Take cover," Daddy yelled as the wind rushed down the bayou with an eerie roaring.

"The canopies are coming loose!" Aunt Colleen shouted. "They'll come right through the windows if we don't get them down."

Daddy sent T-Boy to the water's edge. Balloons and crepe paper and wedding bells had blown clear to the dock. Two empty food trays were floating on the murky water on their way to the cove.

"I'll pick up the trays and the trash," I volunteered, wanting to make sure T-Baby was okay in the storm. He was probably hiding under the elephant ear leaves, the safest place for him, but I still wanted to see for myself.

Daddy grabbed me by the shoulder. "T-Boy can do that. I need you to check on your mamma. And try to get the screens back in the windows as fast as you can."

"But I want to—"

"I need your help with Mamma, Livie," Daddy said, gripping my arm. "Thibodaux can't do it, only you."

This was what I'd been dreading; I just didn't think it'd happen this soon, but I knew I couldn't disobey him. Maybe *checking* on Mamma wouldn't be too hard. I didn't need to get very close for that.

As I pounded up the steps, the flimsy screen door whipped right out of my hands, slamming the side of the house and splintering the wood of the doorjamb.

Inside the galerie bedroom, Crickett was huddled in the middle of our bed, a pillow around her ears. "I hate thunderstorms." Her eyes filled with tears and I didn't blame her. The wailing wind sounded like a crying child. "It's going to give me bad dreams. I want Mamma to rock me."

Her words pricked at me. I'd never liked bad storms, either, the thunder and lightning, the howling wind that sounded like a monster was at the door or trying to crawl down the chimney.

"Mamma used to rock me, too," I told Crickett. "Let's get busy and close these windows on this side, and then we'll climb into the rocking chair and give each other courage until the storm blows on by, okay?"

My little sister slid off the bed to help me and slowly nodded. I realized that I'd comforted Crickett at the same time that I'd given myself the last memory of Mamma I needed for the list. And it was a good one.

Hurriedly, I pulled out the notebook, jotted it down in the final spot, and then added Mamma's Christmas joyfulness and the dancing anniversary last summer on lines seven and eight. I closed the notebook and hugged it to my chest. There, I was done. I had all the memories for the healing spell complete.

"What's that?" Crickett asked, watching me.

"Um, just a memory notebook. I'll show you tomorrow, once this storm is over. Now leave this window cracked open in case the wind gets worse," I added. "I'm going to fix the windows in the living room and be right back."

The front room was a mess. The wind had blown over a lamp and cracked it clean in two. Papers from the tables were on the floor. Even the figure of Jesus hanging from the cross had fallen from the mantle onto

Mamma's bed, but the statue hadn't broken. It was lying quietly by her hand. How strange. Without touching her, I picked up the statue and set it back on the mantle. As if He were watching over her.

The curtains billowed like sheets on a clothesline. I hurried to put the screens back into the open windows, but it was hard to fit them into the grooves. My hand started to throb and then I saw that I'd cut myself. I sucked on my finger as I pulled down the glass, leaving the windows open a couple of inches to keep the pressure from building inside the room. Then I looked at Mamma.

Her beautiful pink dress was splattered with rain and mud; even her hair was damp and tangled. Wet leaves had been sucked through the open windows and stuck themselves to the sheets and the pillows, but Mamma was lying there, mouth flopped open, like there wasn't any storm at all. How could she lay there as if nothing was happening?

"Livie!" Crickett squealed from the galerie.

"I'll be there in a minute. I'm still checking on Mamma."

"Livie!" Crickett called again. "T-Boy just came up the porch screaming bloody murder about something. We have to go back outside, and I'm going to help him."

"You ought to stay inside!" I yelled back. I heard them mumbling and whispering about something, bumping around in the bedroom, and then they were gone.

I ran to the windows and watched Daddy and Aunt Colleen run around the yard, taking down the canopies and stacking chairs. The lanterns swung from the clothesline so fierce I was certain they'd break. I couldn't see any sign of Crickett and my cousin. Where did they go?

Part of me wished I could be out there with them, rescuing the wedding presents, getting soaked and laughing with them, but I had to stay inside because Faye was gone now.

I gulped back the tears, knowing that I was just feeling sorry for myself. Watching over Mamma was now my duty, my obligation. Like a price tag for hurting her.

I'd done everything I was supposed to, just like Miz Allemond had told me. I was working on the faith part, but doubts crept in all the time. My seed of faith wasn't even as big as a grain of sand yet—not even a speck of dust—let alone the size of an actual tiny mustard seed.

Going back inside the galerie bedroom, I unbuckled my dress shoes and laid them inside the box around the tissue so they wouldn't get scuffed up. Maybe someday Mamma would see me wearing them, if I hadn't grown another size by then.

I hiked a pair of jeans up my legs and pulled a shirt over my head, feeling sad that the wedding was over and I wasn't going to look that pretty again for a long time. Then I wondered if T-Jacques thought I was pretty even when I wasn't wearing a dress and Pink Frost lipstick.

I got on my hands and knees to look for my sneakers under the bed and lifted my head again. Something was different about my bedroom. Something was missing. My heart hit my ribs with a deep thud. The corner by the wardrobe was empty. My twenty-two was gone.

That's when I heard the shots down by the cove.

Chapter 16

I KNEW I SHOULDN'T LEAVE MAMMA ALONE IN THE house, but when I heard Aunt Colleen slam through the front door I didn't wait a second longer. Wind gusted as I raced down the slope of the lawn. Thibodaux had my gun in his hand and was waving it in the air. Next to him, Crickett was on her knees, splashing in the water at the bank's edge.

T-Boy had taken my gun without asking. He was going to pay big-time.

When Crickett and T-Boy saw me, they froze, looking guilty as heck.

"What's going on?" I shouted.

Tears slid down Crickett's face, mixing with the rain. She was soaking wet and trembling, her skin white with goose bumps.

T-Boy quickly tossed the shotgun on to the lawn as if he didn't want to be caught holding it. I lunged for him and he shouted, "Take your hands off me!"

Crickett was tugging at my shirt. "Livie, the poor T-Baby."

Her words were a punch in my gut. "No!" I shouted. I didn't want to hear her say that. I was so afraid I was going to lose it right in front of them, so I lifted my fist to sock Thibodaux instead. "Did you shoot something? Did you shoot T-Baby?" My voice wobbled, but I used my anger to keep me from sobbing. "So help me, I'll shoot you!"

He gave a shrug and wouldn't answer.

"Tell me where he is!" I screamed.

Crickett started to blubber, pointing at the elephant ears along the banks of the cove. "Over there!"

"I don't see nothing!" I ran along the bank where the cypress grew thick, the spot where I'd first found him. Plunging my arms into the murky water, I pushed back the carpet of hyacinths.

I hated the wind, the rain, the choppy water, the leaves and debris flying through the air. I wanted to scream at it all to get it to stop. If only I'd come down here sooner when I heard those two kids muttering secrets in the galerie. If only Faye was here and taking care of Mamma, I would have kept my eye on my stupid cousin. If only. There were too many if onlys to count.

I thrashed at the water, trying not to slip in the mud as Crickett started blubbering even louder. I wanted to plug my ears. I didn't want to hear anybody else's grief. Only mine mattered because T-Baby belonged to me.

Yanking purple blooms and plants straight out of the water, I threw them behind me and then I spotted him — T-Baby floating farther upstream, on his side, his little legs limp.

I crawled along the bank until I reached him. The baby alligator had been shot in the head, close to his right eye, but he wasn't dead, not yet. His skin was torn and splintered and his dark eyes rolled back in his head. He made an eerie gasping noise as he tried to breathe and stay afloat.

Getting on my stomach, I reached both arms into the water and lifted him out. I laid him on the grass and stroked the ridges along his tail. "Don't die, T-Baby," I told him. "I'll get Daddy to fix you up right good. Just hang on, please hang on until he gets here."

Crickett and T-Boy stood there, watching, staring. "Go away," I yelled. "Just go away!"

"It was an accident!" Thibodaux said. "We were just practicing. We didn't aim for that stupid alligator."

"No," Crickett contradicted. "You came up to the house scared because there was a gator moving in the water."

"No, I didn't!" T-Boy yelled back. "You shut your mouth."

Crickett started crying harder. "You thought it was going to crawl up on the lawn and eat you."

I stared up at Thibodaux. "You shouldn't have had my gun in the first place. You just took it! You don't know nothing about shooting guns, you ignorant Montana boy!"

Thibodaux's face crumpled and he burst into tears. Then he turned and ran to the house, sniveling all the way. He was only nine. A stupid baby boy.

Crickett knelt beside me. She reached out to pet T-Baby, one finger stroking the top of his head. "I'm sorry, Livie. I didn't know he was so little. I thought there really was a gator in the water going to get us."

I wasn't going to let her off the hook, either. "You should have got Daddy. You shouldn't have let him take my gun! You should have stopped him. You should have said T-Baby was *mine*!"

My little sister looked stricken, tears streaming from her eyes. "Do you hate me, too, Livie? Do you hate everybody?"

Her questions rattled me bad. Why would she even say that? I didn't hate anybody; they all hated me.

Then Crickett started crying even harder. No, I didn't hate anybody, I just hated everything that kept happening to everybody I loved. I hated Faye leaving. I hated Daddy going crazy. I hated what happened that day when Mamma had fallen into the water because of me. Mostly I think I hated myself. Even though I didn't want nobody to see me cry, the tears started coming down my face harder and faster than they had in all these weeks put together. I'd never known crying could hurt so much.

I hated losing Mamma and I was scared I was going to lose Daddy, too. And now I was losing T-Baby for no reason at all.

Lying next to the baby alligator, I put my face close to his and stroked his tiny head, kissing the ridges on his tail, trying to comfort him as he slowly died.

His eyes stared into mine and his breath came in small gasps. He'd stayed in the cove close to the house because I'd kept him there. I hadn't turned him loose into the open swamp where he'd have been better off and could have found other alligators, maybe even his own lost mamma. And now I couldn't do anything to help him. I'd done wrong to him.

The grass was soaked, and there was mud on my cheek. The wind howled around me, the rain poured down like someone had broken the faucet, but all I wanted to do was turn back time. Turn back the last hour. Turn back the clock to three months ago. I'd do everything different if I could.

Thibodaux was right. I could hold and touch and kiss a reptile, but I couldn't touch or kiss my own mamma.

A moment later, Daddy was next to me, his knees in the mud, his hand on my back. When I glanced up, I saw that Aunt Colleen had followed him down to the dock.

She put a hand to her chest. "My Thibodaux did this?"

"He thought the alligator was going to attack him," Crickett explained. "So he shot T-Baby."

"Well, better now than later," Aunt Colleen said with a sniff. "That alligator would have grown into an eight-footer and taken Livie's arm off one day, and then where would we be? Better put him out of his misery."

"Have a heart, Colleen," Daddy said.

Aunt Colleen stood up straight and her voice shook. "Sometimes I think I'm the only one here with a heart! Livie's carrying on over a wild animal more than her own mother. An *alligator*, no less! No one thinks about what's best for Rosemary. I don't understand this family at all."

Aunt Colleen's wild words hung painfully in the air.

Daddy pulled at his face with both hands and gave a long sigh. "Colleen, I do appreciate your help, and it pains me to say this, but I'm not sure if this is working having you here. We don't see eye to eye anymore."

Aunt Colleen wavered as if she'd been punched. "You're going to kill your poor wife if she doesn't have proper medical treatment. And you can't even see it! You are one stubborn man, J.B. Mouton."

Daddy didn't refute her. "Guess I am, but at the moment, we ain't talking about Rosemary's condition. After Thibodaux's reckless behavior with a gun, I think it's best if you go on up to the house and leave Livie alone."

Now Aunt Colleen was crying. Her makeup streaked down her face and her nice dress for the wedding was soggy and ruined. She looked like she was about to say something else, but instead she let out a gulping sob and ran back up the lawn.

I didn't like seeing my aunt crying like that. For the first time, I felt sorry for her, and it made me realize how hard Mamma's sleeping sickness was for her, too. Both she and Daddy loved Mamma and wanted to help her, but the strain was getting to them, getting to our whole family. How much longer could we go on like this?

I held T-Baby even tighter. Thunder cracked overhead and a fresh torrent of rain pelted the yard. Water danced on the surface of the bayou, but I didn't care how wet or miserable I got because my baby alligator was worse off than I'd ever be.

"Let me have a look-see," Daddy said.

He examined the baby alligator, testing his limp legs, then turned on his pocket flashlight to peer closer at his skull. Daddy shook his head. "Sugar Bee, I think he got brain damage. His right eye ain't working. Or his legs. I don't think he can feel me touching him."

"What do you mean?" I knew perfectly well what he meant, but my brain didn't want to register it.

"He's in pain, honey. He ain't gonna heal. We better help him go."

"It's not fair!" I cried. I wished I could take my alligator's pain and transfer it to myself. Losing both Mamma and T-Baby seemed more than I could endure. There were no healing spells to fix Mamma, and no way to fix the holes in T-Baby.

"I know, Livie girl," Daddy said. "Death ain't never fair. Not when it's someone we love."

Rain dripped off his chin, and I could see lines of pain in his face, like they'd been etched by a knife, but my daddy still had compassion for me and my pet. That just made me cry all the more.

Aunt Colleen was watching us from under the porch light, T-Boy blubbering like a nincompoop. Like T-Baby had been *his* pet. Aunt Colleen shushed him, soothing him, holding him.

Crickett sat down on the lawn next to me crying with a fresh torrent of tears. I gave her a look, feeling aggravated at her dramatics, but that just made her bawl even harder.

"All right now," Daddy said. "No need to carry on. Crickett, you go on inside."

Daddy rubbed my back, letting me hold T-Baby for as long as I wanted. His gray hair was wild from the wind and his wedding clothes were drenched through, but he stayed by me, and didn't complain a single second. And that's when I started hoping that maybe he'd still love me even if I told him the truth about Mamma and the accident.

"How you gonna do it?" I finally asked, wiping my hand across my nose, but everything was so wet, it didn't help at all.

"I ain't gonna tell you how, Livie girl, but afterward we'll give him a good funeral."

I kissed the top of T-Baby's head, wanting to comfort him. I tried to speak, just to tell him I was sorry for not taking better care of him. "I should have done better for you, T-Baby," I whispered, "and I'm sorry."

Daddy touched my shoulder. "You ready, Sugar Bee?"

I shook my head, my throat so plugged up with a lump I couldn't swallow right. Rising from the mud, I placed T-Baby in his arms, then I ran past the house, past the vegetable garden until I reached Mamma's art cottage. Sitting down on the step by the door, I waited to hear the inevitable shot from Daddy's gun.

At the last minute, I stuck my fingers in my ears and shut my eyes, putting my face down on my knees and crying until I didn't think I could cry any more for as long as I lived.

A few minutes later, Daddy found me. "So this is where you got to. Where do you want to put him until we can bury him?"

He'd wrapped T-Baby in a blanket and put him in a cardboard box.

"Can I put him in my room for tonight?"

Daddy rubbed his jaw. "Sure, honey. I guess if he's inside he'll be safe from any wild animals. Tomorrow we'll give him a nice service, okay?"

I nodded, wiping my face and tasting salt and bayou mud on my mouth.

"Go on and get ready for bed. I'll be in soon as I finish storing the wedding stuff in the shed."

Crickett was already asleep, crashed across the bed in her nightgown, dirt smears still on her cheek. The house was dark except for a lamp next to Mamma's hospital bed. I could hear water running in the bathroom. Must be Aunt Colleen cleaning up.

Two black streaks of mascara had run down both sides of Mamma's cheeks. The lipstick Faye had applied was faded, too. I was supposed to have cleaned her up when I came inside. 'Course, I hadn't had the nerve.

Mamma's pretty pink dress was wet, leaves plastered all over the bodice and skirt. I thought back to the day I'd slipped into Mamma's closet and snipped a loose thread from the bottom hem. The dress from daddy. A dress that was all about love.

How silly it looked now with wet, soggy leaves all over it. How stupid! And Mamma just lay there, like she enjoyed lying in a wet dress with mascara all over her face.

"Can't you hear nothing?" I cried out, reaching over to shake the metal bed railings as if I could wake her up by sheer will. "A big old cyclone could carry you off and you wouldn't even know it. You wouldn't even care! Don't you *want* to wake up? You look stupid, your hair and dumb old makeup all ruined. And you just stay asleep! *Always* asleep."

As I shook the bed even harder, Mamma's body began to rock back and forth, her hair spilling across the pillow.

"Livie!" Daddy's voice thundered from the doorway.

I quickly pulled my hands away. There was a horrible, awful silence as we stared at each other. The disappointment in his eyes hurt worse than a knife in my chest. "I ain't trying to hurt her, Daddy, I promise!"

It was too late for hospitals or *traiteurs*. It looked like my mamma was going to stay in a coma forever, and now my daddy knew how wicked I was.

Words started coming out before I could stop them. "I never meant to hurt her, but I did! I did hurt her—in my pirogue. I've been so scared she'd never wake up again. That I hurt her forever. I've been wanting to smash that pirogue and burn it—just like you burned up that stump."

"What are you talking about, Livie?" Daddy stepped closer, grasping my shoulder, confusion on his face. "What happened to your pirogue paddle—the one I made for you last summer? Tell me the truth this time."

I looked down at the floor. "Hid it in the shed. I been poling ever since."

"I noticed that. Now I want you to tell me the truth, even if you think it's going to hurt me. What do *you* think happened to Mamma?"

I glanced at Mamma lying on the bed, and I could still see the whole thing. Mamma lying facedown in the swamp, arms and legs splayed out crooked, her hair floating on the surface like dancing lily pads, red blood fluttering out from her head like red Christmas ribbon.

When the dark red blood began to spread across the top of the water, I was terrified an alligator would smell the blood from down the bayou and come eat her. Faye screamed for an ambulance, and then Daddy came running from the shed and jumped into the bayou to pull Mamma out himself. But he hadn't seen the accident, nobody had, but me.

"We was supposed to go to the beauty parlor after we delivered dinner to Mrs. Hebert, and I told her I hated her."

His rough, warm hands were on my head, stroking my hair as I started crying again. I could feel the coarseness of his shirt as he pulled me onto his lap and wrapped his arms around me, rocking me like a baby.

"She told me to go back to the dock. That I didn't appreciate anything she did for me. I was so mad I stood up and rocked the boat and then I started swinging the paddle to get her to listen to me."

"Livie," he said. "I know you'd never purposely hurt your mamma."

"Oh, Daddy, I hit her head with the paddle and she fell out! Mamma almost drowned! But I never thought she'd get a coma."

"Livie, I want you to listen real good." My father's voice was low and deep and he looked real serious as he made me raise my head to look at him. "That tiny paddle of yours ain't nowhere near strong enough to knock a person out and put 'em into a coma. What's more, even if you tipped her out of the boat on purpose, Mamma was a good swimmer. You hearing me, Sugar Bee? What hurt Mamma was hitting her head on that monstrous, rotting cypress stump. That's where the gash come from and all them stitches, not from that lightweight, bitty paddle."

"But, Daddy——"

He held up his hand. "Just keep listening. For years, I promised Mamma I'd take that stump out and I never did. Mamma's coma is *my* fault, not yours."

The room around Mamma's bed whirled like I'd been blindfolded, spun around, and set loose again. I felt my body shaking, as if I was going to fall right over on the floor. My daddy had sucked that stump up out of the bayou mud, chopped it to smithereens, and then burned it in a bonfire to get rid of his own guilt.

"This whole thing with Mamma is my sin. I'm just hoping that when she wakes up she'll forgive me."

I felt as if my daddy had just taken my transgression, put it on to himself, and redeemed me.

"If I hadn't tipped the boat——"

"An accident, just an accident," Daddy said. "Mamma knows that."

"She has to wake up so I can tell her how sorry I am for all the things I said that day."

Daddy grabbed me up in his big arms. "The good thing is, Livie girl, you don't have to wait for Mamma to wake up. You can tell her that any time you're ready."

Chapter 17

AUNT COLLEEN SPOKE FROM THE DARK HALLWAY.
"Some strong, hot coffee would do us all a bit of good, don't you say?"

The clock on the mantle struck once. Wind howled around the eaves, but the house felt safe and warm again. Everybody was inside and the windows and doors were shut tight.

My aunt had been listening to us talk, and I wasn't sure how I felt about that. Seemed like she liked to stick her nose and her opinion into everything, but now that the truth was coming out, maybe that was a good thing.

"Don't think anyone's going to sleep much tonight except the little ones," Daddy agreed.

"I laid a blanket over Rosemary when I came in," Aunt Colleen said. "However, she still needs to be dressed for the night."

I watched my daddy take Mamma's hands in his. "She feels warm enough for a few minutes. I'll get out of these sopping clothes while you make the coffee, Colleen, then I'll get Rosemary ready for bed. Bet I've brought half the bayou into the house with me."

The sharp words between my aunt and my daddy at the cove seemed to have disappeared. I wondered if maybe grown-ups had an easier time arguing with each other and then forgiving. I was still a long ways from forgiving Thibodaux, but another uneasy thought struck me. I wanted to be forgiven and loved despite what I'd done to Mamma. Did that mean I had to forgive T-Boy, too, despite what he'd done?

Aunt Colleen was at my side. "Livie, I'm sorry about Thibodaux and the shotgun. He shouldn't have taken it, and I'm sorry he killed T-Baby. I had no idea how much that alligator meant to you. What I said was wrong, and I'm sure I hurt your feelings. Would you forgive me?"

I was so surprised at her words of apology I didn't know what to say, especially when I'd been thinking mean things about her only a minute earlier. Then my mind flooded with memories of Aunt Colleen since the day she'd arrived. All those times she'd gotten on her

323

knees praying for Mamma, cooking and tending to all of us, staying up all night.

I'd left her in a puddle of water that very first day, and yet she'd forgiven me and never brought it up again. Aunt Colleen had even left her own sick husband in a hospital to come help Mamma. My aunt was a bundle of contradictions.

"Please?" Aunt Colleen pleaded, putting her arm around me in a hug.

I nodded and a fresh set of tears burned my eyes.

"I know you've had a sore festering inside your heart all these weeks. I could see it in your face every single day, in all your actions, but I couldn't figure out what it was. I hope we can all start healing now."

The healing spell. Was it too late for it to work? Maybe my faith would grow even more now that Daddy and Aunt Colleen knew the truth and I knew they still loved me. I wondered if all that fear and guilt had been keeping the seed from taking root in the first place.

"Think you'll be okay for a minute while I go in the kitchen?"

I hesitated.

"I'll be close if you need me," Aunt Colleen added.

I listened to the sound of water running and the strike of the match to light the gas stove for the coffeepot, then I looked down at my wet clothes and felt a mess, too. My eyes were crusty from all the crying I'd done, and my nose was sore from wiping it so much.

Hovering over the bed, I watched my mamma breathe. I was closer than I'd ever been before. I suddenly missed Faye so much. There was so much to tell her, and it had only been a couple hours since she and Travis had left. I wanted to tell Faye about the storm, T-Baby, the truth about Mamma.

Then I remembered what Faye had told me just before she left on her honeymoon. "Talk to Mamma, Livie, just talk to her."

I'm sure it wasn't what Faye had in mind, but maybe that's what I needed to do. Tell Mamma the whole story and add that to my healing spell.

"Remember that day, Mamma," I started and immediately felt my throat closing up on me. I cleared it and brushed back my wet hair, leaning two inches closer over the white hospital sheets so she could hear me better. "I'm sorry I argued with you, that I told you I hated you. I didn't mean to knock you out of the boat or hurt you. Well, I wanted to hurt you with those awful words because I was so dang mad. I wanted you to know how I felt, but I didn't mean to give you this sleeping sickness. I just wanted you to love me like you love Faye and Crickett and Daddy. That's all."

I was sure I didn't have any tears left after T-Baby died, but they started sliding right out of my eyes again and spilling down my chin. "Oh, Mamma, I'm sorry," I said, but the words came out so soft, I wondered if she could hear me through the coma. "I truly am sorry, and I want you to forgive me. And I want you to wake up." I paused and stared at her, and it felt like I was begging God, too. If anyone could help her wake up, He could. He had to hear our prayers, hear Aunt Colleen's rosary, know that I was sorry and wanted to do better. I wanted Mamma to know it, too.

"I do love you, Mamma, even though we spend most of our time mad at each other." There was a queer flash inside my chest and that ugly knot of guilt started to break into pieces. At that moment, I loved my mamma more than I ever had before, and I felt it rushing through my whole heart. I kept talking, telling her about Faye's wedding party, her beautiful beaded dress, Aunt Colleen rescuing the cake from the bakery, and the storm. Then I told her about T-Baby and finding him in the cove under the elephant ears and how he'd follow me in my pirogue. I finished with the story of how he'd died that very night, but I left out the bad parts about Thibodaux, and I was proud of myself.

"Me and Daddy are going to give T-Baby a proper funeral tomorrow morning, Mamma. Once the rain stops."

I'd never been this close to her in almost three months. The faint blue veins in Mamma's pale skin looked like a spider's lacy web. The pulse in her neck throbbed as I noticed the green leaf stuck to Mamma's chest. I sucked in my breath when I saw that on top of the leaf, a daddy longlegs spider sat in a teardrop of rain, just sitting doing nothing.

The spider began to move. All those long spindly legs unfurled themselves and started walking across Mamma's chest. In a moment, that spider would crawl up Mamma's neck and onto her face. I couldn't let a nasty spider crawl right over Mamma's mouth and nose and eyes, but how could I get rid of it without touching her?

Carefully, I reached out and grabbed the spider by one of its legs. It dangled from my fingers as I walked to the front door and threw it onto the woodpile by the side of the porch. When I got back, I gasped to see that a roly-poly bug had crawled out from under that darn leaf next. It was about to work its way inside Mamma's dress, right down her bosom.

Fast as I could, I grabbed a piece of newspaper and scooped the bug onto the paper to set him on the windowsill. Boy, I was getting good at this. I could fix things for Mamma without ever touching her at all. Holding my breath, I bent over one last time to pick up the wet green leaf off Mamma's chest.

I aimed for the stem so I wouldn't have to touch Mamma's skin, but just as my hand got close, her left arm suddenly lifted into the air. The next moment, Mamma's hand brushed at her chest as if she was trying to find the leaf herself. *Like she could feel it there.*

Mamma's mouth began to move, her lips fidgeting. Her eyelids fluttered as if she was dreaming. The next instant she grabbed me by the wrist.

I let out a shriek. Mamma's clasp was strong!

My heart exploded inside my chest. Immediately, Mamma's other arm rose and picked the leaf right out of my fingers. She held her hand out to the side and dropped the leaf to the floor.

"Mamma," I whispered as the hair on my arms rose like I was on fire. *"Are you waking up in there?"*

Her grip loosened and then her hand dropped back to her side, all floppy again, like nothing had ever happened. But I knew better. My mamma had moved. She'd *moved.* Had grabbed me like she'd known I was standing right beside her. Like a corpse suddenly coming to life in its grave.

My mother wasn't dead at all. Her hand had felt warm, *alive*. Her skin was smooth and soft, just like I remembered. Not cold and lifeless like I'd imagined all this time, but warm and cozy and real.

"Daddy!" I shrieked. "Aunt Colleen!"

He burst from the hallway into the living room. "What is it, Sugar Bee?"

"Mamma—" I started, but my voice choked up so much I couldn't speak.

Aunt Colleen raced in from the kitchen and quickly checked Mamma over, taking her pulse, listening to her breathe, feeling her face. "She seems fine, honey."

I stared at them. "Mamma moved."

"Of course, she moves at times," Aunt Colleen said. "Sometimes the coma makes her agitated, even though she's completely unaware. You know that."

"No, Mamma moved *on purpose*. Lifted her arm and grabbed my hand. She even dropped that oak leaf right there."

Daddy and Aunt Colleen stared at the floor where the wet green leaf lay. My aunt's face turned white.

"Colleen, do you think . . . ," my daddy began.

My aunt's eyes filled with tears. Her chin quivered and she put a hand to her mouth. "J.B., I don't dare hope."

"I gotta hope," Daddy said. "Livie, you sure? You positive?"

I nodded. "I'm positive, Daddy."

Aunt Colleen brushed at her eyes. "It might have just been a rigid muscle reaction. I don't know . . . but if she's close, maybe we can try to get her back again."

I watched Aunt Colleen start to rub Mamma's arms and legs. She pinched her fingers, tickled her feet, snapped her fingers against Mamma's palms.

Then Aunt Colleen got right in Mamma's face. "Rosemary, come on and wake up. We know you can do it. Do it again. Give us a sign, honey. Move your arms, just one little toe. Please, Rosemary, do it for me. Do it for J.B. Wake up for your baby girls."

She worked on Mamma for several long minutes, and I tried as hard as I could to will her to wake up, too, with everything I had inside me.

"Wiggle a toe, flutter a finger, anything, Rosemary," Aunt Colleen urged.

I held my breath, but there was nothing.

Aunt Colleen turned away and burst into tears.

Daddy put his hand on her shoulder while I stared into the silence. Mamma was lying completely still again. There was no sign that she'd ever moved at all.

In the bayou, thunder cracked once more. I could hear the rain beating against the roof.

The teakettle in the kitchen began to whistle, and Aunt Colleen gave a start. She took out a handkerchief, wiped her eyes and blew her nose with it, then balled it up in her fist.

The kettle got louder.

"Go on and get that," Daddy told her. "Livie and I will dress Rosemary for the night. Won't we, Sugar Bee?"

My eyes flew to his face and I felt my stomach give a jump.

My daddy smiled at me, slow and sure, like he was confident in me. Like he had *faith* in me, and I just had to start using the faith in myself that was already there.

I moved my head up and down, agreeing to help him. "I'll bet Mamma's cold in that wet dress."

"You sure you're both okay?" Aunt Colleen asked.

Daddy waved her away, and she hurried off to the kitchen to save the kettle. "You do Mamma's shoes and stockings while I get the dress off."

"Okay," I whispered. Fact is, I'd just saved Mamma from the danger of bugs and insects and moldy leaves. Taking off her shoes was no sweat. And Mamma had already touched me once tonight. She wasn't clammy or cold or scary or like a corpse at all, so I didn't have to be afraid anymore. I knew I couldn't hurt her, either. Anything I did would be helping her to get better.

I took a step forward and pulled off her white sandals, sticking them under the hospital bed. Daddy unzipped the dress and slipped it over her head and then I could wriggle Mamma's white stockings off her hips and down her legs. They were damp, but not too bad. The dress was worse.

"We'll have to take this to the dry cleaner's tomorrow," Daddy murmured. "How 'bout you go get a couple of dry towels, Livie, while I finish up Mamma's slip and underthings?"

I was relieved he'd do the hard part. By the time I got back with warm towels from the dryer, Daddy had Mamma under a sheet again. I took the wet clothes into the laundry, hung up the dress, and stuck the rest of her stuff into her own basket for washing.

Back in the front room, while lightning flashed across the windows, I took one of the towels and dried Mamma's arms and hands and neck while Daddy did her legs and feet.

Once again, her skin was warm and soft, just like when she'd grabbed my arm and made me yell. Mamma felt normal. She was still my mamma, no matter what happened.

"I can do this," I said to myself, then realized I'd said it out loud.

"I always knew you could, Livie girl," Daddy said quietly.

Tears stung my eyes as I helped him lift Mamma's neck and shoulders to slip her favorite nightgown of soft buttercup yellow over her head. I remembered that ugly green hospital gown with the stupid floppy ties that always stayed loose. That was a long time ago. I wasn't sure I was the same girl anymore. That girl wouldn't have helped Daddy right now. She would have run away. That girl didn't have seeds of faith and love growing inside her. I could feel them swelling stronger, sprouting, taking root inside my heart. I gave a glance at the healing string on Mamma's ankle and knew it was mending the pieces of my heart back together again.

After Daddy had laid a light blanket over her, I got the brush from her dresser and combed out Mamma's hair. The coma had lasted long enough that it needed a trim. I wondered if I should do it or wait for Faye. No, my sister wouldn't be home for a long time. I'd do it tomorrow. I'll bet I could cut it straighter than mine turned out.

"I think she's done," I said, looking up.

"You done beautiful, Sugar Bee."

I chewed on my lips, desperately wanting her to move again, to turn her head toward me and open her eyes. I wondered if I could stand waiting like this without going crazy.

"What'll we do if Mamma stays like this forever?" I asked.

Daddy reached out and swallowed me up in his big arms. "We'll just keep on loving her. And lovin' each other."

Chapter 18

HOURS AND HOURS LATER, I COULDN'T GET MY mind to stop playing pictures of the wedding, and T-Baby's death, and Mamma grabbing my arm. Felt as if I'd had a year's worth of crying in a single day.

I couldn't go to sleep, so I finally just got up. The silence of the house enveloped me like a caterpillar's cocoon, tight and dark. The thunder and lightning had gone down the bayou, but it was still drizzling, a steady patter on the roof.

An image of Mamma's art cottage shot into my mind. Had anyone checked it during the storm? I didn't really want to go out in the middle of the night, but I couldn't let Mamma's beautiful paintings get ruined if a window had been left open.

The ground was squishy under my toes. Rain dripped from the leaves of the oak trees overhead. The studio was peaceful; windows shut tight, no problem at all. I didn't know why I'd been worrying.

Snapping on the flashlight, I picked my way around the canvases propped along the walls waiting for framing. I stopped at the easel and studied myself standing in the pirogue. The picture was beautiful and mysterious in the light of the flashlight. It gave me shivers thinking about my mamma out here painting it for me, thinking about me in just this way, with the things I liked best. I loved it.

The next instant, my heart jumped clear into my throat.

In the lower right corner, a little baby alligator had been painted swimming among the elephant ears near the bayou bank. I held the flashlight higher. The alligator had the same tiny black eyes and the dark emerald coloring I knew so well. Even the bumps on his back, his teeth and claws — it was all so perfect, so real.

A tear inched down my cheek. It was like I'd been handed a gift. Mamma had added T-Baby to the painting so I could remember him.

But that couldn't be right. The first time I'd seen

the painting, there was no background and no baby alligator. T-Baby had become my pet long after Mamma fell into the coma. Weeks later. Mamma didn't know anything about him.

My brain felt rattled, as if someone had taken my memories, dropped them out of my head, then poured them back in. Sinking to my knees, I shone the flashlight over every inch of the picture. My skin prickled.

All the empty penciled spaces had been filled with color: the greens and blues and browns of the bayou and the house set back from the banks. There was the dock, the cove, and the rippling chocolate-colored water.

Mamma had painted me looking off in the distance down the bayou road — the road I loved so much. Mamma knew me better than I ever thought she did.

All the pieces of my questions started falling into place. The painting was the miracle I'd been waiting for. I stared at it, amazed at how real T-Baby looked as he swam happily in the cove. I lay down on the floor with my flashlight, not wanting to stop looking at it, wishing I could feel close to Mamma out here forever.

Next thing I knew, gray light was coming through the cottage windows. I yawned so hard my mouth cracked. I felt like I'd turned a hundred years old overnight.

In the pale morning light, the painting looked just as good as ever. The best part was, it was still real; I hadn't dreamed it. I raced out of the cottage and back to the main house, jumping up the porch steps to the galerie bedroom. Crickett was asleep with a finger in her mouth, and I raced past, not stopping until I was in the front room.

Daddy looked up from his spot in the chair beside Mamma. "You're up bright and early, Sugar Bee," he said groggily. He'd never gotten ready for bed and now his hair was messed up, unshaven whiskers decorating his chin.

I rubbed my eyes. "I couldn't sleep."

Daddy scratched at his face. "Guess it's time to finish cleaning up the yard. That storm last night—whooee— what a surprise."

He got up from the hard-backed chair and I heard his knees creak. "Think I'll hit the shower. How about making a batch of fresh coffee? I'm sure Colleen would appreciate some hot brew when she gets up. Keep an eye on your mamma for a bit, too. Pound on the door if you need help."

"Okay, Daddy."

He shuffled off to the bathroom, and after the door closed, I couldn't stand it any longer. I crouched over Mamma and stared at her, willing her to open her eyes. I summoned up all the faith I could from deep down in my gut. "Mamma, I know you're in there. *I know it!*"

Not a flutter of her eyes or a lifting of a finger. A salty tear slid down my nose. The rock started to settle inside my chest again, but I didn't want it there anymore. I wasn't going to let it stay, but how could Mamma fall back asleep so deeply after she'd been awake? Was there something else I needed to do?

I dragged myself into the kitchen and poured a measure of coffee granules into the pot, added water, then lit the gas stove. From the galerie, I heard Crickett rolling over in bed. The sound of feet came from Aunt Colleen's room.

Wedding evidence was everywhere. Dirty dishes stacked with dried food. Leftover wedding cake lay in crumbs on the counter. One single pink sugar rose sat untouched on the last edge of the cake. It was so perfect and beautiful, I didn't want anyone to eat it or throw it away.

In the galerie, I perched on the edge of the bed to pull on my shorts, gazing at the box holding T-Baby. Yesterday had been a wedding. Today there would be a funeral.

I yanked a shirt over my head and caught a very strange sight on the floor. A set of muddy footprints came up the outside steps, crossed the screened-in galerie floor right past my bed, and then walked into the kitchen. They had to be my own footprints coming back from the cottage just now, but a funny tickle began to rise in my stomach.

The mattress squeaked as I got up to follow the footprints. Tiny bits of mud had dried on the carpet. They must be mine, or were they? I got to the hospital bed and watched Mamma's breath rise and fall.

With all the wedding makeup scrubbed off her face, her hair falling across her shoulders, Mamma looked young, like a girl again.

My heart pounded as I picked up the blanket. There were speckles of mud on the bottoms of her feet. Just like mine.

Then I saw something else. The knotted string on Mamma's ankle was gone. The string had been there when Faye dressed Mamma for the wedding, because I remembered seeing it, and it was there last night, but now it wasn't.

I ran back into the galerie bedroom.

Crickett opened her eyes and brushed the flyaway hair out of her face. "Morning, Livie."

I could hardly get the words out. "Did you cut that string off Mamma's foot? Or take it off? Or anything?"

Crickett shook her head. "You told me never to touch it, and I haven't. Promise, cross my heart and hope to die, stick a needle in my eye."

I ran back through the house. Aunt Colleen came yawning down the hallway. Her long silver hair wasn't even combed yet.

"Aunt Colleen, you saw that string on Mamma's ankle, right?"

"What are you chattering about, honey? It's too early in the morning."

"A string. On Mamma's foot."

"Oh, yes, I knew Crickett had done that. Playing some sort of game, I imagine, hearing us talk about *traiteurs* long time ago."

"But did you ever take it *off*?" My hands were shaking now, the back of my neck sweaty.

"No, I couldn't bring myself to disappoint her, but maybe we better take it off and find a fresh length."

I didn't wait to hear any more. I raced to Thibodaux's bedroom.

"Who is it?" he grumbled when I knocked.

I didn't wait to be invited in. I pushed open the door as he lifted his head from the pillow to stare at me suspiciously. "Go away."

"T-Boy, I promise I will never bother you again," I told him, and I nearly died of shock at what I was saying. "And I promise I will be a good cousin to you from now on. You can even come frogging with Daddy and me next time. But answer me the God's honest truth — so help you forever."

Thibodaux sat up in his pajamas. His red hair stuck straight up like a rooster's comb.

"My mamma had a string on her right ankle. Did you ever mess with it? Ever take it off or cut it or anything?"

"Are you crazy?" T-Boy said. "I'd never touch your mamma."

Those words were good enough for me.

I raced back to the front room, getting down on my hands and knees to look under the furniture, the couches and chairs, the newspapers lying scattered. I even searched the entire kitchen. The string was nowhere in sight. It was truly gone.

Aunt Colleen poured herself a cup of coffee, then dragged out the toaster and plugged it into the wall. "How about cinnamon toast with the leftover bread?"

"That's my favorite," I said as I banged out the front door. I flew across the grass straight to the art cottage again. Strong sunlight now spilled through the windows. A breeze spattered raindrops from the trees overhead, like a dog shaking off water from a bath.

I conducted the same intense search throughout the little cottage. I looked in every corner, behind the easels and empty white canvases and paint bottles and under the table and chairs. And when I finally found it, I laughed for not looking there first.

The knotted string was wrapped around the handle of the very same paintbrush I'd used to pluck the bristle from, the item that went into the first knot when I came back from Miz Allemond's house. The brush was sitting back in the metal can with all the other art brushes, clean, soft, and ready to use.

I picked it up, touching each small healing knot. The rosemary crumbled dry in my fingers, but there was the strand of Mamma's hair and the thread and the necklace chain and the buttons and the hyacinth blossom and the smell of Mamma's favorite perfume. Even T-Baby's little broken tooth was still attached. A wave of fresh tears spilled over my cheeks as I put the brush with the healing string into the pocket of my shorts, clutching the handle so it wouldn't fall out.

I stood on the step outside again, teardrops running down my cheeks, and yet I felt like laughing, too. Funny how smiling and crying could happen at the very same time.

Daddy was sitting at the dock. Confetti from the wedding lay strewn around the pilings. The lines on his face were deeper and longer than ever, but he squinted up at me and patted the grass for me to sit down. "What a night, Sugar Bee. I'm dog-tired. Kept having the strangest dreams. I swear your mamma was talking to me last night. Even felt her squeeze my hand. Maybe you were right when you saw Mamma move. That's what I keep thinking. Isn't that the most peculiar thing?"

When I heard those words, the last pieces of that heavy rock in my chest melted clean away, and I knew it was finally gone for good.

"I keep wondering if I dreamed the whole thing, but it sure seemed too real to be a dream." Daddy gave me a sideways look. "What's up, Livie girl?"

I splashed the water lapping against the bank with my big toe, swirling my feet until the tiny bits of mud washed away. Washing me clean. The sins and the guilt and all the bad that had come with it were finally gone.

Forgiveness was sweeter than I'd ever imagined. Hope was turning into faith. In fact, they were so close they could almost be the very same thing. Or they could be, if I let the tiny seed keep growing inside me. I realized that faith could fix a broken heart. Faith was the glue that held it together. That was part of the miracle.

"Daddy," I said.

He pressed my hand inside his big palms. "Yes, honey?"

I wanted to shout the words for the whole bayou to hear, but the lump in my throat made it so I could only whisper, *"I think Mamma's about to wake up."*

What would my daddy say to such crazy words?

"I know, bébé-child, I know," he murmured, gazing out over the chocolate-syrup waters. "I know she's gonna wake up, just like I know that sun is rising above the cypress. Never knew anything so strong in all my life."

"It's gonna be soon," I added because there was something inside me that just *knew*. I moved closer to Daddy, feeling his warmth, taking note of all the little things that I loved—Daddy's scratchy beard; the chipped metal button on his shirt grazing my cheek; his thick, bent fingers as he stroked my arm.

I started making plans. I'd find my hidden paddle in the shed, row out to the crawfish traps, and get a big load to deliver down the swamp to Miz Mirage Allemond. I owed her a debt that still needed to be paid, but I'd have to leave it on her porch because she wouldn't accept any gifts that were called a payment. Giving crawfish was something I could do better than anybody else.

I grinned as I thought of something else — an invitation for Crickett and Thibodaux to come along and help deliver my load.

When I glanced over, I saw that my daddy had tears running down his cheeks. Long wet streaks running through the wrinkled crevices all the way to his chin. But his face was serene, and I realized that his tears were good tears, not sad ones any longer. The tears of relief that come after a long, harsh rain. The kind that come after so much sorrow, when everything feels lost but will soon be found again.

"It's gonna be soon," I said again, and I liked how the words sounded. I liked the truth of those words because I'd already figured out that Mamma didn't have the sleeping sickness anymore. The coma was gone. After weeks and weeks of aching heat and sadness, Mamma was truly sleeping now.

The mud on Mamma's feet. The knotted healing string on the paintbrush. T-Baby inside the painting. All those things were Mamma's doing, proof she really was waking up.

"Sun's getting higher," Daddy observed in his slow, quiet way. "You ready to say good-bye to T-Baby?"

I slowly shook my head, and then looked into my daddy's dark blue eyes. "No, but I guess I have to." He rose to his feet and held out his hand to help me up from the dock.

While Daddy retrieved a shovel from the shed, I went to the galerie and got the box from the floor by my bed. Setting it on the bedspread, I stole a glance under the cloth tucked around T-Baby's body. It was hard to look at him, the limp tail, the small, helpless little legs, and the messy hole in the side of his head. I turned away, digging my knuckles into my eyes, then picked up the box.

We walked to the far side of the cove and I chose a spot under the shade of the big oak.

Daddy dug first, using his strength to break up the tough grass and get the hole started. When he hit soft dirt, he handed the shovel to me and let me dig for a few minutes. We shared the shovel and shared the silence, too. Somehow, I knew we were both thinking about helping Mamma to come back to us, and hoping she'd be okay, but also hoping we could face whatever might happen, good or bad.

"Think that's big enough, Daddy?"

"I'll square up the sides," he said, taking the shovel and finishing the hole with a grunt. He leaned on the shovel and peered down to inspect the work.

I thought about how much I hated what a grave looked like. Cold damp soil, lonely emptiness. Tears pushed against my eyelids, and Daddy reached out, bringing me to his chest in a tight squeeze. "It's gonna be all right, Sugar Bee, gonna be all right."

I pulled back, the smell of laundry soap on his shirt filling my nose. "I'm okay," I said as I watched him place the box into the bottom of the shallow grave and give it a gentle pat. "Good-bye, T-Baby," I whispered and the words seemed to scald my throat.

"Happy hunting in alligator heaven," Daddy added softly.

Kneeling on the grass, I used my bare hands to push the pile of damp dirt back into the hole. My fingers got sticky and black with mud, but I didn't care. I swished my hands clean in the bayou, then wiped my nose again while Daddy packed the mound down good and hard.

"Think I'll plant some flowers here," I said. "Maybe some purple hyacinth and an elephant ear or two."

I thought about Mamma preserving T-Baby in the painting forever, happily swimming in the cove and peeking at me through the surface of the water. Maybe I really could be the girl in the painting. The girl my mamma saw.

When Daddy finished the grave mound, a swell of loss and love crashed against my heart like the bayou colliding against our rickety pier.

"You gonna be twelve next week, ain't you, Livie

girl?" Daddy said as I slipped my hand into his wide palm. "Mamma's got something real nice planned for you," he added with a wink.

I patted the pocket of my shorts, making sure the paintbrush was still there, feeling the handle and the bristles stab me in the side.

Sometime during the night, Mamma's own fingers had wrapped the healing string around the paintbrush handle—sometime during those dark hours after the storm when Daddy fell asleep and had those strange and wonderful dreams.

Just like Daddy told me the day of the dress shopping long ago, maybe Mamma and I could have a love that was stronger and deeper than I ever thought was possible. I couldn't figure out how it happened, but I felt the hugeness of that knowledge bursting up from my toes, rising straight to my heart, and filling everything in between.

Maybe the healing spell from Miz Allemond wasn't just for Mamma. Maybe it had been meant for me all along.

Recipe for a
Healing Spell

Take one strong, flax string, quarter-inch thick

Tie nine individual knots along the length, top to bottom

Dip in holy water blessed by the priest and

Hang to dry in a moss-laden oak.

Find nine items belonging to the person who needs healing, then

Fasten each object into a knot good and tight.

Search for nine lost memories—

Good ones to stay within your heart—

Bad ones to leave in the swamp forever.

Wrap the string around the ankle of the one you love

Apply faith and prayer in good doses, then

Wait for the knotted string to fall off.

That's the day the healing spell will be complete.

Acknowledgments

MY JOURNEY WRITING *THE HEALING SPELL* WOULD NOT BE COMPLETE WITHOUT THANKING THE MANY PEOPLE WHO HELPED ME ALONG THE WAY WITH CRITIQUES, ADVICE, AND CONSTANT CHEERS:

Cindy-Rae Jones, a Southern woman in heart and mind (if not current location) who is also a wise and amazing road trip cohort. Thank you for your treasured friendship and always inspiring me.

✳ Barbara O'Connor, for an astounding thirteen-year e-mail friendship and for always knowing exactly the right thing to say. ✳ Frances Hill, for reading Livie's story after Write Fest and making me stretch one more time. ✳ Poetry connoisseur Kelly Fineman, for her generous tutorial in prose and rhythm. ✳ Shannon Reed, for answering my many medical questions. ✳ Jennifer Park, who lifted me up in countless phone conversations, and who fell in love with Livie so much she wouldn't return the manuscript and kept it as a "souvenir." ✳ Rusty Little, my endlessly supporting husband and first critique-r, who missed his bus stop because he was gulping down the last chapter to find out what happened. ✳ Huge thanks go to my amazing cheerleaders, Special Agent Tracey Adams and the entire Adams Literary family. ✳ To my extraordinary, insightful, and all-around immensely talented editor, Lisa Sandell, as well as everyone at Scholastic who loved Livie's story and helped bring her to life between these pages, thank you so very much.

✳ And last, but never least, to the Fems critique group, for always being there: Carolee Dean, Nancy Hatch, Marty Hill, Kris Conover, and Neecy Twinem.

About the Author

KIMBERLEY GRIFFITHS LITTLE IS THE AUTHOR OF A dozen short stories that have appeared in numerous publications, as well as the critically acclaimed novels *Breakaway, Enchanted Runner,* and *The Last Snake Runner.* She is the winner of the Southwest Book Award.

She grew up reading a book a day and scribbling stories, while dreaming of seeing her name in the library card catalog one day. In her opinion, the perfect Louisiana meal is gumbo and rice, topped off with warm beignets, although crawfish étouffée runs a close second. Kimberley had her own bayou adventure, narrowly escaping an alligator encounter when the curious gator climbed out of the bayou and crawled up onto the lawn, straight for her.

Kimberley lives in a solar adobe house near the banks of the Rio Grande in New Mexico with her husband and their three sons. You can visit her at her website at: www.kimberley griffithslittle.com.

Critically acclaimed author
Kimberley Griffiths Little
weaves a haunting story of
friendship and family
in her next novel,
CIRCLE
OF
SECRETS.